Dear Reader,

When I first heard Judy Collins sing a song she wrote called "The Blizzard," I knew I'd experienced something special. Set in the Rocky Mountains of Colorado, the song tells the story of a woman with a broken heart who, stranded during a blizzard, finds comfort in the arms of a stranger.

Pure romance, don't you think? I promised myself that someday I would write a story that would start where Judy Collins's song ended. My heroine is a down-on-her-luck country-western singer who unexpectedly ends up caring for an abandoned infant while traveling through the Colorado mountains. There's a snowstorm and a sympathetic sheriff and one night of passion. And then the story begins....

I hope you enjoy this book as much as I enjoyed the music.

*Kristine Rolofson*

## KRISTINE ROLOFSON,

author of over thirty novels for Harlequin Books, lived in the mountains of north Idaho for twelve years before returning to New England in 1987. A Rhode Island native, she now resides in the same town where she spent her childhood. A mother of six and married for thirty years (at age eighteen she married her high school history teacher!), Kristine writes about family life in many of her books.

After years of combining writing with other jobs as a waitress, wallpaper hanger, secretary and seamstress, Kristine's only job now is writing, which she loves to do. She also loves to travel, especially to the London flea markets, and will use any excuse to board a plane and head anywhere in the world. She also collects scrimshaw, antique jewelry and Western history books and can often be found prowling through New England secondhand stores.

---

### Books by Kristine Rolofson

# babies
## & BACHELORS USA

# Kristine Rolofson
## Jessie's Lawman

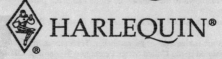

# HARLEQUIN®

TORONTO • NEW YORK • LONDON
AMSTERDAM • PARIS • SYDNEY • HAMBURG
STOCKHOLM • ATHENS • TOKYO • MILAN • MADRID
PRAGUE • WARSAW • BUDAPEST • AUCKLAND

Dedicated to Pat and Chet Farrell
for the afternoon on the Berthoud Pass, with special
thanks to Pat for her patience in Colorado while I
researched this book and ate my weight in boiled shrimp.

**HARLEQUIN BOOKS**
225 Duncan Mill Road, Don Mills,
Ontario, Canada M3B 3K9

ISBN 0-373-82254-5

JESSIE'S LAWMAN

# 1

"DON'T WORRY. The music won't bother her none," the teenager said. She leaned her head back and closed her eyes, dismissing the woman who had stopped to give her a ride.

Jessie Carter glanced down at the truck's floor. "Her" was the sleeping baby tucked beneath the hitchhiker's feet. She switched off the radio anyway. The songs reminded her all too painfully of Mick, and she didn't want to be reminded that he hadn't loved her enough to take her with him when he got his big break. The rowdy bar songs were sung by men, the same singers who'd rejected her soft ballads as not "hard-edged" enough.

She didn't want to sing along with the songs anymore, didn't want to feel the humiliating envy for every songwriter whose latest creation was being broadcast over the Colorado airwaves. Maybe heading to Nashville wasn't such a hot idea. A broken heart, wounded savings account and thirteen-year-old Datsun pickup truck weren't the smartest combination.

"My name is Jessie," she offered into the silence. "What's yours?"

"That's not important, is it?" Her accent was pure country.

"Guess not," Jess agreed. Jess turned her attention back to the empty interstate in front of her. The girl beside her wasn't much company. She'd picked her up sixty miles ago, unable to resist the skinny teenager holding a bundle that was obviously a child. The young woman, her stringy blond hair covering her cheek, slumped in the passenger seat, her child tucked in a dirty blanket at her feet. Not the safest way to transport a baby, but Jessie certainly couldn't produce an infant safety seat from the jumble of her belongings loaded in the truck bed. There was nothing she could do except pray the tiny baby would be safe.

And wouldn't cry. Which was another good reason not to listen to the country-western selection on the radio. Silence filled the truck, except for the rattle of the right-hand door, and the odd clatter in the vicinity of the glove compartment.

Jess let another mile pass before she spoke again. "Where did you say you were headed?"

"Anywhere, don't matter much."

Not exactly the answer Jess expected, but she wasn't surprised. "I'll take you as far as Denver," she offered, knowing she'd probably relent and take her all the way to Tennessee if that's what the girl wanted. Besides, she hated to admit that the isolation was finally getting to her. She'd tried to ignore the aching, homesick feeling in her stomach, but there was no doubt the loneliness of this trip was starting to take its toll.

Jess drove without speaking while the baby slept contentedly at her mother's feet. Another hour passed, putting another sixty-five miles between her and Mick, but finally hunger set in. She'd eaten half a bag of potato chips instead of stopping for lunch, and the young hitchhiker had eagerly finished the rest.

"I'm going to stop for dinner at the next town we come to," Jess said, glancing toward her passenger.

The girl's eyes narrowed. "For how long?"

"Long enough to eat something hot. You're welcome to join me."

"I'll think about it."

*And maybe I'll think about how long I'm going to put up with you.* Jess turned her attention to the road ahead and started watching for signs.

An hour later she faced the girl in a red vinyl booth in a restaurant called Buffalo Joe's. The town looked as if it supported a pretty big tourist business. The storefronts were freshly painted, ready to welcome the winter season's first skiers.

The hamburgers had been thick, the fries hot and the coffee strong, so Jess was content. When the baby woke and began to complain, the young woman ordered a glass of warm milk and poured it into a bottle for her.

"I thought babies drank formula."

The woman shot Jess a defiant look, a look that said, *Mind your own business, lady.* "I have to get some more."

"We can stop at a grocery store after we eat. I think we passed one on the way in."

The girl shrugged, propped the baby's bottle up with the blanket and slid out of the booth. "I need to pee."

"I'll watch the baby," Jess assured her, even though the girl hadn't asked. She moved over to sit beside the infant and smiled into her wide blue eyes. The little girl smiled around the nipple of the bottle, letting a trail of milk dribble out of the corner of her mouth. Jess grabbed a napkin and wiped it before it soaked her collar.

"You have to pay attention to what you're doing,"

she cooed, leaning closer. Then she realized that this little girl needed a fresh diaper.

"You're a messy girl, aren't you?" Jess hoped the baby would smile again. Her little eyes crinkled at the corner in the most enchanting way. "Your mommy will be right back, then she'll change your pants and buy some proper food."

The bottle was empty, so Jess set it on the table and awkwardly picked up the child. She thought babies needed to be burped, if she remembered correctly. Her baby-sitting experience years ago had been brief, only long enough to earn the money to buy a guitar.

Jess smiled at the memory. She'd ordered it from the Sears catalogue and taught herself to play it.

Now she was broke, burping a stranger's baby in a quiet Colorado town on a Sunday afternoon. Mick would laugh if he could see her now; he'd tell her she was too softhearted and too accident-prone. The kitten she'd rescued from a dumpster had scratched her, a nasty wound that had required a trip to the doctor. A scraggly Christmas tree had fallen over under the weight of only half the ornaments. And the drummer who'd needed a place to stay had run off with the VCR and the grocery money.

There was a pattern here, Jess thought, patting the baby's back until a satisfying burp erupted near her shoulder. "What a good girl you are," Jess crooned, and the baby gurgled.

The waitress came by to clear the plates and drop off the check, but there was still no sign of the hitchhiker. Jess hoped she wasn't sick in the ladies' room. She tucked the baby against her shoulder. "Let's go find your mommy."

But mommy was nowhere to be found. Jess searched

the bathroom, then hurried through the restaurant. There was no sign of the girl.

"Miss!" someone called behind her.

Jess turned as the waitress hurried toward her, holding the check. "Yes?"

"You forgot this," the woman snapped, clearly suspicious.

Jessie took the check. "Have you seen a young blond girl? She had dinner with me, and now I can't find her."

The waitress shook her head. "You check the bathroom?"

"Yes." Jess switched the baby to her other shoulder and fumbled in her purse for her wallet. She managed to take out a twenty-dollar bill, handed it to the waitress and followed her over to the cash register.

"Cute baby you have there."

"She's not mine," Jess explained. "She belongs to the girl who ate with me."

The waitress, an older woman with graying hair, shook her head. "That one looked like trouble."

"She's a hitchhiker," Jess admitted. "I picked her up this morning. She had a backpack and a baby and I felt sorry for her."

"Maybe she's waiting for you in the car."

"I hope so. What kind of person would leave her baby with a stranger?"

The waitress shrugged. "I've seen all kinds, honey."

Jess returned to the booth long enough to pick up her jacket and the baby's blanket, and leave a tip on the table. Then she hurried toward the restaurant door with the frightening feeling that the hitchhiker had disappeared, leaving her with the check and the child.

From the door Jess could see the parking lot and her truck. The cab was empty.

Jess stopped the waitress once again. "Is there a sheriff or a police station in this town?"

The woman shook her head. "You can call the county sheriff's office for an emergency. They usually send someone out pretty fast."

"What about the state police?" Jessie felt the first stirring of panic. She had to find the hitchhiker fast, before she disappeared completely. The little girl gurgled in her arms. "I have to find the baby's mother. And soon."

"I can get you the phone number," the waitress offered, glancing at the child. "I've heard of strange things, but this one beats all."

Jessie looked down at the baby and held her a little closer. Maternal instincts she hadn't known she possessed made her want to protect the child left in her care. "We'll find your mommy," she promised the wide-eyed baby. "Don't you worry about a thing. Jessie Carter is going to take care of you."

DAN MACADAMS SWIVELLED on the stool and studied the storm raging beyond the windows of Gussie's Diner. The neon lights that rimmed the eaves cast an eerie orange glow on the falling snow, and the fluorescent lights inside appeared even brighter compared to the dark night. The last customer had left an hour ago, taking his offensive cigar and leaving the jukebox quiet. A peaceful change, Dan thought, tired of rollicking country tunes blasting against his eardrums. Gus, the diner's cook-manager-owner, switched on the radio and the two of them listened to the weather report and the road conditions.

"Stay home," the announcer ordered. "The state police are closing all passes now that it's dark. And if you absolutely have to go somewhere tonight—and I don't know why you would—make sure you have chains on."

"I'm glad I took your advice and sent the girls home early," Gus said, refilling Dan's coffee mug. "It's no night to be crossing the pass."

Dan nodded. "Yeah. And I'm glad I'm finally off duty, though I could still get a call."

"Anyone who needs the sheriff will have to wait. You could never get off the mountain." Gus pointed toward the parking lot as headlights approached. "Here comes someone else. Whoever it is must be glad they made it this far."

Dan picked up his coffee cup and turned to face the door. He didn't like surprises. He waited as the headlights darkened. He could barely hear the car door slam over the roaring wind.

The diner's bell tinkled a warning as a young woman with a bundle held protectively against her chest attempted to wrestle the door open. Dan reached the door in three strides and held it against the wind while the woman entered the warm room.

"Thank you," she said, her voice rich and melodic. She pushed her hood back and a dusting of snow fell to the vinyl floor. Yellow hair tumbled down to her shoulders, and her gray eyes were framed in dark, snow-tipped eyelashes. She had a perfect heart-shaped face, and the tawny skin indicated a woman who liked the outdoors. Dan held his breath, waiting for her to speak again. But she looked down at the squirming bundle in her arms instead, and flipped back the blanket to reveal the round face of a baby.

"My God!" He couldn't believe it. "You brought a child out in this weather?"

"I didn't exactly have a choice," she responded, and there was an undercurrent in her words that caused Dan to take a closer look as she headed to a nearby booth. She was no giant, probably around five feet three inches tall, and compact. She wore a heavy parka, blue jeans and worn cowboy boots. An oversize leather purse was slung across her shoulder, and a plastic grocery bag hung from a delicate wrist. Her mittenless hands clutched the child whose pink-flowered blanket needed washing.

Dan frowned and returned to his stool. He assumed she was in some kind of trouble. Only a desperate fool or an ignorant traveler would attempt to cross the pass in weather like this.

Dan picked up his coffee mug and turned to watch as Gus headed toward the booth. The woman laid the baby on her back beside her on the seat and set a full baby's bottle on the table top. Dan leaned back and waited. There was a mystery here, he could feel it.

"Bad night," Gus said to her, wiping his hands on his apron.

"I didn't know what I was going to do until I saw your light. I can't believe I made it this far."

"You're lucky you didn't slide right off the mountain," Gus agreed. "You must be hungry. I've turned the grill off, but I can fix you a nice open-faced turkey sandwich. With gravy and mashed potatoes."

"That sounds perfect. And could you put this in hot water for me?" the woman asked, holding out the bottle.

The cook took it gingerly. "Sure."

"Thank you so much."

"Sure. Cute kid you have there."

The woman hesitated, then answered, "I think so, too," then turned to the baby and started fumbling with the child's clothing.

Dan turned away. He leaned over the counter, grabbed the carafe and refilled his coffee mug.

"Nice lady," Gus murmured, holding out an empty mug for Dan to fill.

"Maybe." Dan lowered his voice. "I'm going to run a plate check on her truck. What fool would be out in this weather?"

Gus shook his head. "I thought you were off duty."

Dan shrugged. "Just thought I should check it out."

"You think too much," Gus said, and took the coffee over to his only other customer.

"Heading for Denver?" Dan heard Gus ask.

"Yes, or at least I thought so. Until the storm." The baby began to wail.

"I'll get that bottle," Gus said, hurrying toward the kitchen.

Dan was unable to resist the urge to turn around. The woman looked at him and smiled ruefully.

"Sorry," she said. "She should be quiet in a minute."

"No problem. Babies cry. What's her name?"

Again, the hesitation. "I call her Jane."

"Jane," he repeated. "That's an old-fashioned name."

She didn't answer. "Is this the only road between Granby and Denver?"

"Yes. This will take you to the interstate. From there you head east."

Gus returned with the bottle. She took it and awkwardly shook a few drops on her wrist to check the temperature of the formula. Satisfied, she popped the nipple into the baby's mouth, cutting off her wails, then turned back to Gus. "Have you seen a blond hitchhiker, a young girl, in the diner tonight?"

Gus put his beefy hands on his hips. "I don't think so. What about you, Dan? You seen anybody like that?"

Dan thought for a moment, then shook his head. "Not since I've been here. Why?"

"It's not important. I'll take care of it in Denver."

It was the perfect time to tell her he was the sheriff of this county, but Dan sensed there was something wrong here. She was a beautiful woman, no man with eyes could argue with that, but until he could identify what bothered him, he was going to wait.

The wind continued to howl around the building. Gus served the woman a plate piled high with turkey and potatoes and refilled her coffee mug as the snow fell relentlessly past the windows. The lady with the baby wasn't going anywhere, Dan knew, at least not until the roads were plowed, and that might not be until morning.

He had plenty of time, and no place to go. Except home. His warm bed, new mystery novel and glass of brandy would have to wait a little while longer. Thank goodness.

He wondered what her name was.

JESSIE WONDERED who he was. A large man, he looked as if he was accustomed to being in charge, the kind of man who expected to know exactly what was going on all the time. Handsome, too. Dark, curly hair and a strong, square face. Surprising green eyes under heavy brows had eyed her with curiosity. Quite a combination, with the wide shoulders and powerful arms covered by the diamond-patterned ski sweater.

But not threatening, she realized, covertly watching him as she pretended to look past him to the heavy snow falling outside. He'd gone outside once, and she thought he'd gone home to his family. But he'd returned, his dark hair covered with snow, his expression calm. He had refilled his coffee mug, she noticed, and no longer chatted with the cook. There was a strength about him, a power that had nothing to do with his height or the size of his shoulders. He folded his newspaper and shoved it aside, then turned and moved toward her.

"Mind if I join you?" he asked, his question almost a demand.

"Well—" she eyed the sleeping infant by her side "—if you whisper."

His gaze flickered past her to the baby, then returned to settle on Jessie's face. "I'll be quiet," he assured her, and set his coffee mug on the table before sliding into the booth. "Did you think you were going to make it to Denver tonight?"

She sipped her coffee. "That was my plan, yes."

"The pass has closed."

"Are you sure?"

"It's on the radio."

"But I have to get to Denver." She heard the desperation in her voice and took a shallow breath. It wasn't this man's problem that she was stuck with a baby abandoned in a restaurant miles back, that a hitchhiker had disappeared, that Mick didn't love her anymore and no one famous bought her songs to sing. She felt the tears well up in her eyes and blinked them back.

She absolutely refused to shed any more tears over anything or anyone.

"Are you in some kind of trouble?"

Jess glanced at the baby by her side, and the child opened her eyes and gurgled with contentment. "I have a very big problem," she confessed. The safe feeling she had didn't mesh with the man's cautious expression or the suspicious glint in his eyes.

"If it makes you feel any better, I'm the deputy sheriff around here." He reached into his back pocket and pulled out his wallet. He showed her his identification. Daniel J. MacAdams. "I'd be glad to try to help you any way I can," he offered.

Relief shot through Jess, and she smiled. "Then you're just the man I want to see."

"I am?"

She continued to smile. "I tried to get help in Granby, but there wasn't anyone there who could help me. That's why I need to get to Denver, you see, because then I could talk to the state police and get some help."

"Help with what?"

"With Jane. That's not her real name. I just called her that—like Jane Doe, you see."

He frowned. "She's not yours?"

"No. Her mother—at least I think it was her mother—left her with me at a restaurant and disappeared."

Dan took a pad and pen out of his pocket and leaned forward. "What's your name?"

"Jessie. Jessica Carter."

"Middle name?"

"Lynn."

"Birthdate?"

"September 19th." He waited. She added, "1965," and watched as he carefully wrote down the numbers.

"So you're twenty-seven."

"Barely." She waited for him to smile, but he didn't look up.

"Your address?"

"I don't have one right now. I'm, uh, moving."

He finally looked up, a frown marring his handsome features. "Moving where?"

"I'm not sure." She didn't want to tell him she couldn't decide if she should go home to Chicago or take the final, biggest risk and head for the Music Capital of the World. "Nashville, I think. I'm a songwriter and singer."

The deputy stared at her, his pen forgotten in his hand. "You're a songwriter?"

She nodded, wishing he didn't look so incredulous. "Well, I'm *trying* to be."

"I've never met a songwriter before. What kind of songs do you write?"

"Country-western, ballads, that sort of thing." He seemed to be waiting for her to continue, so she added, "I play the guitar a lot and the piano a little."

"Would I know any of your songs?"

She lifted her chin. "Not yet. Although there might be one out soon. I cowrote it with a new band called Muleshoe."

"Sorry. I've never heard of them."

"You wouldn't, not yet. They're touring with Clint Black now, as his opening act." She watched as he made a note of that on his pad.

"And the name of the song?"

"'Dancing with Heartache.'" He wrote that down, too. "It will be on their new album."

"I'll look for it," he promised, his smile warming her. Then, as if he remembered what he was supposed to be doing, he turned back to his notebook. "Your last address?"

Jess gave him the address of the apartment in Los Angeles she and Mick had shared for the past eighteen months. She didn't give him any details.

He wrote it all down, then looked up at her and waited. "Maybe you'd better start at the beginning."

Jessie did, telling him as much as she could remember about the scraggly-haired young woman who had hitched a ride with her that morning. Dan MacAdams asked a lot of questions, sometimes twice, until he seemed satisfied that he understood.

"Did anyone see her leave the restaurant?"

"Not that I know of. The place was pretty empty. It was around three, so it wasn't exactly lunchtime."

He thought for a minute, tapping the pencil against the pad. "There's not much around that town, except the road. Where would she have gone?"

"I don't know. She just disappeared."

"And you didn't stay in town, in case she returned. Why not?"

"I did, for a while. I had to buy formula and diapers at the grocery store. But then I thought she—the baby's mother—could be out there on the road trying to get a ride and maybe I could catch up with her. I figured if I didn't find her, I'd take the baby to the state police in Denver. I called them, but the connection was so bad I gave up trying to explain."

Gus came over once to refill their coffee mugs. "I'm going to shut the place down," he announced. "You two can stay as long as you want. Miss—" he turned to Jess "—you and the baby are welcome to spend the night here. I'll be back at six. I don't expect anyone else to show up, but I'm going to leave the outside lights on just in case."

"Good idea, Gus," Dan said. "Thanks. I'll turn the coffee off when I leave."

"Thank you," Jess echoed. "I guess I'm not going anywhere tonight after all."

"That's for damn sure," the deputy muttered. He turned to the cook. "You're taking the cash with you?"

Gus nodded. "Yeah." He turned back to Jess. "There's pie in the cooler. Help yourself," he added before shuffling into the back room.

In half a minute the overhead lighting in the diner went off, leaving a gray glow from the kitchen as the only illumination. Jess blinked, relieved that the bright fluorescent lights were no longer burning her eyes. She was tired, tired from moving, driving and baby-sitting. "He sleeps here?"

"There are cabins on the ridge behind the diner," Dan informed her. "You probably couldn't see them through the snow."

Jess chuckled. "I was lucky I could see the diner."

Dan looked back at his notes. "It's been hours since the hitchhiker disappeared."

"Yes. I was so sure I would see her on the side of the road. But the longer I drove, the more I wondered if she deserved to have this baby. I mean, what kind of person would leave her baby and just take off?"

The sheriff gave her a long look, then shook his head. "I've seen worse things, lady." He stood up and slid out of the booth. "I'll go out to my Jeep and call this in. There's not going to be many people out in this storm, though." He grabbed his heavy jacket and slipped it on. "Do you need anything from your truck?"

"There's a blue bag and a pillow in the back. It's not locked."

"Fine."

"Thanks. I really—" Jessie stopped as he pulled the door open and disappeared into the storm. She shivered as the wind hit her neck and checked Jane to make sure she was comfortable. The baby had drifted off to sleep again, blissfully ignorant of the drama taking place around her. How old was "Jane"? Certainly not a newborn. Four or five months old, Jessie guessed. Maybe the sheriff, who probably had children of his own, would be able to guess better than she.

Aside from raising those dark eyebrows of his, he'd shown no surprise at her story, thank goodness. Jessie touched the baby's cheek with a gentle finger. So soft. And so very vulnerable. She turned to look out at the storm raging outside. What would have happened to them if she hadn't seen the lights of the diner and pulled off the road into the parking lot? She'd been so grateful to be alive that she'd rested her forehead on the steering wheel for a long moment and had whispered a heartfelt prayer of thanks. Those last miles had been hell. And being responsible for a life other than her own had made the drive through the mountains even more terrifying. She hoped the energy the coffee had given her was enough to make it through the night. She had a baby to care for, and the booth didn't look as though it would make a very comfortable place to sleep.

She'd sleep tomorrow, when this was over.

The sheriff pushed the door open, the tinkling bell above the frame announcing his return. He set her duffel bag and pillow on a nearby chair and turned to check the door.

Jess felt the same relief she'd experienced when she'd turned into the diner's parking lot. This man would help her. She and Jane were safe from the storm, and a sheriff's deputy would now find Jane's mother. She watched as he took off his coat and shook off the snow, then hung it on one of the hooks by the door. He ran his fingers through his snow-dusted hair and stomped his boots on the mat to release the snow clinging to the leather. She could tell it was a familiar ritual by the automatic way he performed the simple tasks.

She wondered how long he'd been a deputy. He looked about thirty, as solid as the Rocky Mountains, and about as intimidating. Until he slid into his seat across from her once again. She watched him, noting an ease in the previously tight line of his lips. The cautious expression in his eyes was still there, but without the suspicious edge that had made her uncomfortable when he'd studied her earlier.

As if she'd done something wrong, and hadn't admitted it yet.

"Thanks for getting my stuff," she said.

He pushed his coffee mug off to one side and leaned back. His knee grazed hers for a split second before he readjusted his legs. "No problem."

"Did you talk to the state police?"

"Yes. They'll keep an eye out for your hitchhiker. And tomorrow, when the storm stops, they'll send someone out to Granby to look around."

"It will be too late by then." She glanced at the sleeping baby and back to the deputy. "She could be anywhere."

"No one is going to get far in this storm," he assured her. "Look at you, stuck here on the pass. I still don't know how you made it this far. You're a very lucky woman."

Jessie couldn't help her laughter, but she choked it back in order to prevent waking Jane.

The man across from her looked surprised. "You want to tell me what's so funny?"

"I'm the unluckiest person I know," she confessed, still smiling. "My father disowned me when I told him I wanted to be a musician. I've sold only one song, and that I ended up giving away. My boyfriend, the man I've loved for three years, left me behind when he got his big break, and took another singer with him—a redhead named Debby—and sublet our apartment without telling me. And today a hitchhiker left me with her baby, I'm stuck in a snowstorm, and I think I'm lost."

Dan's lips turned down, as if he was trying not to smile. "Anything else?"

Jessie didn't know whether to laugh or cry. "Yes. I have to use the bathroom. Would you sit beside Jane and make sure she doesn't roll off the seat?"

"You'll come back?"

She couldn't tell if he was teasing or not. "Where else am I going to go?"

# 2

DAN MOVED OVER to the other side of the booth as the woman who said her name was Jessie Carter headed to the back of the diner. Maybe he was all kinds of a fool, but he wanted to believe her crazy story about a hitch-hiking teenaged mother disappearing into thin air.

The baby opened her eyes and flailed her little arms. Her gaze settled on him and, as if she didn't like what she saw, she screwed up her mouth and started to wail. Dan chuckled and leaned over to pick her up, surprising her into silence. The two of them considered each other, the baby making faces as if she couldn't decide whether to scream or smile. He sat her on the edge of the table, keeping a grip under her arms, and gave her a chance to make up her mind.

She smiled.

Dan smiled back. "Hi, there, little lady. You've decided to like me?"

Her smile widened, and drool trickled over her lip and touched her chin.

"I wish you could talk. I have a list of questions that could use some answers." He studied the little girl's face. Blue eyes, button nose, sticky yellow hair. She could use a bath, and a new outfit. The little fuzzy thing she was wearing looked about worn through. "For instance, where did you come from? And who's your mother?"

Jane's mouth made a little O as she stared wide-eyed at him.

"Not going to talk, huh? You're one of those mysterious females, I guess." He almost smiled at her blank expression, then gathered her into his arms and tucked her close to his chest like a football. He slid out of the booth and walked over to the window to see what was happening with the storm. The blizzard had worsened; he could no longer see the outline of Jessie's truck.

He'd checked the back of the truck thoroughly, noting there was no baby equipment, like a bed or car seat, in the jumble of boxes and household equipment piled in the bed of the truck. Two guitars, snug in worn cases, were wrapped in blankets. An amplifier took up much of the space, along with a black, painted rocking chair. He'd checked the front seat, too. The rumpled road maps verified her journey, but he couldn't get the glove compartment open to check the registration.

Headquarters had taken the license plate number, but Betty said the computers were down again. There was no way of knowing the truth about Jessie Carter, at least not until morning.

He'd have liked to believe the gray-eyed woman with the sweet voice was telling the truth, but he'd learned a long time ago that people weren't always what they appeared to be. Still, he decided, turning away from the window as Jessie came back into the room, he didn't mind the company.

She smiled at the baby, with a heart-stopping expression that made Dan swallow hard.

He didn't mind the company at all.

Jess made no move to take the baby from his arms. "Should I make a fresh pot of coffee?"

He didn't want coffee, didn't want to sit on the

booth's hard bench as the wind whipped around the building and snow hid the road. "Sure." He didn't want to leave, either.

"Okay." She went around the counter and quickly assembled a new pot.

"I'd say you've been a waitress," he noted.

She wiped her hands on a paper towel. "I sure have. And a bartender, chambermaid and short-order cook, too. Anything to pay the rent, you see."

"What about singing?"

She went over to the table and collected their mugs, then took them back to the sink and dumped the cold coffee down the drain. "Singing and songwriting never paid the bills, unfortunately."

"It's not easy to get rich and famous?"

Jess shook her head as she wiped the cups dry. "Almost impossible."

"Then why do you do it?"

"I love it," she answered, her voice soft. She sounded almost surprised at her words, and looked past Dan's shoulder at the storm outside. "I love writing songs, love hearing other people sing them. I sit there and listen and know I created something special, something that hadn't existed until I put the notes on paper. Singing is something I do for other people, but writing songs I do for myself."

Jane started to whimper, and Dan turned away reluctantly from the intriguing woman. "What's the matter?" he asked the baby, as if she would answer.

Jess stepped around the counter. "I don't think she's hungry again. Maybe she's wet."

Dan followed her to the booth as the baby started to sob in earnest. "Do you know any lullabies?"

"I guess I'll have to write one." Jessie pulled a box of

disposable diapers out of the grocery bag. "I knew I should have bought a bigger box," she muttered, pulling a diaper from the perforated opening. "Put her down here on the seat. I'll do this as quickly as I can."

He did as he was told. "You know how?"

"I'm learning fast." She managed to unsnap the screaming baby's pajamas and tug her little legs free from the material. "You might want to turn around, Sheriff. This is going to be a messy one."

Dan MacAdams, the man who had tracked two escaped murderers through Berthoud Pass in 1984 and had seen the wreckage of more car accidents than he could count, turned around. With relief.

"I'll get the coffee. And pie," he offered, hurrying away from the booth.

"Get me a couple of wet napkins, will you?"

He could handle that, he figured. He folded six napkins into neat squares, wet them with warm water from the faucet, then delivered them to the booth before returning to slice the apple pie.

"All done," Jess declared after a couple of minutes. "If you'll watch her, I'll get rid of this stuff and clean up."

"My pleasure," Dan said, surprised that he meant the words. Here he'd thought he was in for another long, agonizingly quiet night, and now he was in the company of a very attractive woman who liked to talk to him and a baby who liked to smile at him.

By the time Jessie returned to the booth, Dan had poured fresh coffee and fixed thick slices of apple pie. He'd made the baby a bed on the floor, making certain she wasn't in any drafts, and the child seemed content to lie on her back and look around.

"What a good idea," Jess said, noting the layers of towels cushioning Jane from the hard floor.

"I was afraid she'd roll off that bench." Dan sat down and waited for Jessie to join him before taking a sip of his coffee.

Jess eyed her pie. "I already paid for my dinner. Do we write down what we take?" She looked at Dan and grinned. "You're the lawman. Tell me how we do this."

"Pie's half price at night. You can leave a dollar on the counter."

"Plus coffee money."

"Plus coffee money," he agreed.

They ate in companionable silence for a few minutes, until Jess could no longer stand the quiet. For some reason she liked to hear this man speak. He spoke slowly, as if always measuring his words, cautious about making certain he'd used the correct ones. Unlike Mick, who pelted her with his thoughts, opinions and activities. And she'd hung on every word, she remembered bitterly.

"Tell me, Sheriff, how did you get stuck here tonight?"

He put down his fork and pushed his empty plate away from him. "I didn't." She waited for him to explain. "I rent one of Gus's cabins. I usually eat dinner here after work."

"You mean all you have to do is walk out the door and go home?"

"That's right."

"Then why don't you? I mean, why haven't you gone home?"

"You had a problem. I had to do my best to solve it."

"But you can't," she countered, her voice firm. "So

go home and get some rest. We'll still be here in the morning, and I'll wait to find out what should happen next."

Dan took another sip of coffee, as if thinking it over. "I can't leave a woman and a baby in an empty restaurant in the middle of a storm."

"Sure you can," she insisted. "We'll be fine. I'll curl up right here on this seat, with my trusty pillow. Jane will curl up under her blanket and sleep like a baby." She smiled at her own joke.

He didn't return the smile. "It's not right."

She leaned forward and planted her elbows on the table. "I'm lucky I'm not spending the night freezing to death on the side of this mountain. Compared to that, this place is a four-star hotel."

"Not for a baby."

Jess stood up, as if to shoo him out. "Go home, lawman. Call it a night."

Dan stood, too. He looked down at her with an aggravated expression. His mouth thinned into a stubborn line until he spoke. "Not alone."

She raised her eyebrows. "What?"

"You two will have to come home with me. There's a couch, and a wood stove. It will be a hell of a lot more comfortable than this place." He moved out of the booth and bent to pick up the baby. "We'll wrap her up real tight. It's not a long walk."

Jess hesitated. She knew nothing about this man, except he had the identification of a lawman and he'd been kind. It still didn't seem right to sleep at his house, but it was tempting to think about resting her tired body on some soft couch cushions. Her lower back was stiff after driving all day, and her shoulders were beginning to ache. "But I don't know you."

He looked surprised, as if he wasn't used to having anyone *not* know him. "I've lived here all my life, been a deputy for the past eight years. I've never abandoned anyone in trouble in my life, and I'm not going to start tonight." He picked up the baby and handed her to Jess. "You wrap her up and I'll tuck her inside my jacket." Still Jess hesitated. "Look," he said, gathering up her tote bag, pillow and bag full of diapers. "That baby needs a bath and a warm place to sleep. You can stay here if you want to, but that little girl is going next door."

Jess shrugged her coat on. "Not without me."

Dan hid his smile and went to the door to get his coat.

THE BRUISES, unmistakable oval fingerprint marks, marred the baby's thin arms. Jessie looked at Dan to see if he'd noticed. The grim look on his face told her he had.

"It's as if someone held her very tightly," she said, wondering how anyone could hurt such a helpless human being.

"Held her to shake her, I imagine," Dan replied, a thread of anger in his voice. "Are there any other marks?"

Jess finished undressing the infant and turned her over. She felt sick to her stomach. "I don't see any. Maybe her mother didn't really mean to hurt her."

"Right." Sarcasm tinged the word.

Jess turned her attention to the job at hand. She held Jane carefully and lowered her into the warm water in the sink. "I hope I'm doing this right."

He handed her a bar of soap. "You're doing fine."

"She's not even crying."

"She likes it. Look at her eyes."

Jess bent forward and Jane's little hand splashed water on her face. "Why, you little monkey!" Jane gurgled with happiness as Jess moved the bar of soap over her pink skin. She debated about washing Jane's hair and settled for rinsing it with water; she didn't want to risk getting soap in the baby's eyes.

Dan moved closer. "I've got the towel ready. Just drop her in my arms when you're done."

"Easier said than done," Jess muttered, trying to rinse the soap off the baby's skin without dropping her. She'd given up trying to keep her cotton shirt from being drenched, despite the fact that she'd rolled up the sleeves past her elbows. She leaned closer to the sink and cradled the baby tightly. Jane was about as slippery as a greased pig, only happier. "Go to Uncle Sheriff," Jess said, as she placed the child in Dan's waiting arms.

"Uncle Sheriff?"

She helped wrap the towel around Jane's bare skin. "It seems to fit," she teased.

He almost smiled. "I prefer Dan."

"All right, Uncle Dan. Now what?"

He moved to the couch positioned near the wood stove. "We keep this little girl warm."

Jess followed him to the couch and sat down next to him on the overstuffed tan cushions. As the sheriff had promised, the little cabin was snug and warm, a big improvement on the diner. The walls of its one large room were pine panelled, the floor covered with a worn braided rug. At one end of the room was a small kitchen with a round oak table and two chairs; the other end boasted the wood stove, a leather recliner and the couch. A small television perched on top of an overflowing bookcase near the recliner. Blue-checked curtains covered the windows and blocked her view of the storm, but Jess could still hear the wind.

She shivered, knowing if it hadn't been for pure luck she and the baby would most likely have died in the storm tonight. "Are you still cold? It should warm up in here soon."

Jess turned her attention to the man beside her. He was studying her with a concerned expression. She shook her head. "I'm not cold. I was just thinking about the storm. I'm so glad I made it to the diner before the roads drifted closed."

"You were lucky. So is she."

"You think so? She lost a mother today." Jane rested on his knees, her face peeking out of her towel cocoon.

"And may find her tomorrow, although she'll have to face the county social workers and prove she's a fit parent. She has a lot of explaining to do, including how Jane here got those marks on her arm."

"The baby looks happy enough now."

"Do you have any other clothes for her?"

"No. Just what she had on, and I hate to put that back on her."

"Maybe we could wrap her in one of my T-shirts," Dan suggested. "What do you think?"

"I think we'd better try. She can't go naked until I wash and dry her sleeper."

"I'll be right back." Dan handed her the baby, then disappeared through a door across the room. She assumed it was the bedroom; she heard drawers being opened and closed.

"You're such a good girl," she told the baby. "And you smell so much better."

Jane smiled as if she understood the compliment.

"Aren't you sleepy? Auntie Jessie is starting to get very, very tired. We've had a long day, haven't we?"

Dan's low voice interrupted her. "Try this."

She took the shirt and almost laughed out loud. Four babies could easily fit inside the expanse of white cotton.

"It's clean," he assured her as she hesitated.

"But there's so *much* of it."

He handed her the box of disposable diapers he'd left on the floor. "I don't have anything smaller."

"We'll do our best, won't we, Jane?"

It took longer than she thought to diaper and dress the squirming infant, and the sheriff was no help. He didn't mind holding Jane when Jess was finished, though, giving her a chance to wash out the baby's few clothes and drape them near the wood stove to dry. The lawman's thick boots made a pretty good drying stand and kept the clothes out of the wood chips and ash scattered across the stone hearth.

"She doesn't look sleepy."

Jess straightened and went over to the couch. Jane's wide-eyed gaze followed her. "No, she sure doesn't. She slept in the car all day, so I guess she's not tired."

"As long as she doesn't scream, I guess that's all right."

"You don't have to sit up with us. We'll be fine out here."

"I'm fine. I had enough coffee to keep me up all night." His smile almost reached his eyes.

Jess hid a yawn and watched as Dan stood up and walked over to the window, Jane nestled comfortably in his arms. "It's still snowing." Then he turned back to Jess, who tucked her chilled feet beneath her as she leaned back into the cushions. "Tell me about your songs."

The question surprised her. "What do you want to know?"

He didn't seem in any hurry to sit down again. "How did you start?"

"I made up songs all the time when I was a kid."

"Did you grow up in a musical family?"

"No, not really." He seemed to want her to talk. Jess didn't mind. "We listened to the radio in the car, that was about it. My parents never really understood my wanting to be a songwriter. They tolerated the guitar as long as I kept my grades up in school." She thought for a moment, remembering. "Actually, I think my mother enjoyed the love songs I wrote, the slow ones. My father was disgusted with the whole thing."

Dan moved back to the couch, and laid Jane on the cushion between them after he sat down. "Why?"

"I come from three generations of physicians. Surgeons, not singers." Odd, how her father's rejection still hurt. "As an only child I was expected to pick up a scalpel and carry on the family tradition."

"You picked up a guitar instead."

"Yes. And left home the day I turned eighteen."

He frowned. "You ran away?"

"Not exactly. I went to Nashville with a band. I went back to Illinois once, when my mother was dying of cancer. At her funeral my father told me not to bother coming back again, unless I was going to stay and get a 'respectable' job."

"He sounds like a tough man."

"Dr. Carter is used to playing God, believe me. That was four years ago."

"Then what?"

"The band got a shot at a pretty good gig in a club in L.A., so we headed out there, hooked up with an agent and started making the rounds of the record companies. We stayed in California and managed to pick up plenty of work, enough to pay the rent and repair the equipment, anyway." She left out the part about catching Mick snorting cocaine in the dressing room right before the final show in Tahoe.

"Where's the band now?"

"We split up. They found a new singer, so I packed up my stuff and decided to go back to where I belong."

"Nashville," he stated.

"Nashville."

"And you're still writing songs?"

"Not really. Since I, uh, left the band, I haven't had the heart to write anything. It's as if that part of me is frozen." She looked away, embarrassed that she had revealed too much to a total stranger.

He cleared his throat. "You don't sing anymore?"

Jess saw the disappointment on his face when she turned back to him. "You want me to sing?"

Dan looked embarrassed. "I've always had a weakness for guitar music."

"I'm a little rusty. I haven't picked up the guitar since..." She stopped, unwilling to reveal anything else.

"It won't matter to me," he promised.

"In that case, I'd be glad to—it's the least I can do after everything you've done for me, but I'll have to get my guitar out of the truck." She uncurled her legs and started to move off the couch.

He moved, too. "Stay. I'll get it."

"But..."

He touched her shoulder, sending a current of

awareness jolting between them. His fingers were warm on her shoulder, a warmth that seeped through the thin cotton of her shirt. A smile touched his lips. "You stay here with Jane. She could use a lullaby, remember?"

"I remember." What was the matter with her? She could feel his touch even after he moved away to take his jacket off one of the wooden chairs in the kitchen.

He returned long minutes later, both guitar cases in his grip, the blankets that had covered them draped around his neck. Snow dusted everything, including his dark hair. Jess had the crazy urge to brush it off for him, but she kept her distance and reached for one of the guitars instead.

"I didn't know which one you wanted, so I brought them both." He set them down by the door and tossed the blankets over a chair.

"I should have brought them in sooner. Drastic changes in temperature aren't good for them."

He hesitated. "You want them by the stove?"

"No. The kitchen is fine." She knelt on the rug in front of one of the cases and pulled out her old Gibson while he took off his boots and jacket.

"Why do you have two?"

"One's electric. The other's an old friend."

Dan looked over at the baby, waving her little fists in the air. "Are you sure she can't roll off the couch?"

"No, I'm not sure at all." Jess knelt at eye level with the couch cushions. "Should I put her on the floor?"

"No. I have a better idea." He disappeared into the bedroom and a few minutes later reappeared with a blanket-lined drawer. He set it on the braided rug beside the couch. "This should work, if she's not too big."

"A drawer?"

"You don't think it's a good idea?"

"I think it's brilliant." She watched as he lifted the baby into the box, deep enough to protect her from rolling out and hurting herself. Jane gurgled her satisfaction with her new surroundings and smiled up at Dan. Dan gave her his finger to grip and the baby held on as if she never wanted to let go. Jess watched the exchange between them, envying the infant's simple ability to hang on to the lawman and trust that he wouldn't hurt her.

Jess hugged her guitar closer to her chest and blinked back tears as she remembered holding out her hand to Mick to beg him to stop taking the cocaine that had changed him into a different person, a man she didn't know and didn't like very much.

A man who didn't love her anymore, and hadn't minded saying so.

Dan laughed. "She's a strong little thing, isn't she?"

"And happy, too. I guess babies are tougher than we think."

"At least this one is." Jess met Dan's gaze, and she knew they were both thinking of the bruises on Jane's arms.

"Will she be all right?"

"I'll make sure she will be."

She trusted his promise. Dan MacAdams, lawman, would be capable of keeping the baby safe. He had a certain strength about him that made her want to crawl into his arms for protection and safety. There was a power radiating from him, a sense of being in charge that she had recognized the minute she'd entered the diner. He would take responsibility for Jane's future. She, on the other hand, could drive down the mountain tomorrow and never give Jane another thought.

Which would be impossible, but necessary.

"Are you going to sing?"

Jess blinked, realizing she'd been lost in thought while this man waited to be entertained. She cleared her throat. "Sure," she managed, running her thumb down the strings. She moved to the couch and sank into the cushions. She quickly adjusted the strings, then strummed again until she was satisfied. "All set," she announced, raising her gaze to his. He'd taken his seat in the worn recliner, his stocking feet pointed toward the wood stove.

Jane lay nearby, still waving her arms, despite the odd nightgown that covered her body. "Do you think she's warm enough?"

"She's fine," Dan assured her. He crossed his ankles and put his arms behind his head. "Play," he ordered, then softened the instruction with a "Please."

Jess grinned. "I love an anxious audience."

"You've got one, lady."

"Well, let me know when you've had enough," she cautioned. "I can start at Bob Dylan and work through the decades to Vince Gill. I'll throw in a few original tunes just to keep you guessing, okay?"

"Okay," he agreed, knowing he'd agree to anything she wanted to sing. Just to hear another voice in the cabin, to make contact with another human being, he'd agree to almost anything. She could play "Row, Row, Row Your Boat" and he'd think it was wonderful.

And so she began. Dan listened to her sing an old folk song and knew he was in the presence of someone with enormous talent. Her voice was simple and pure, with an effortless ability to hit high notes and low, and Dan sat entranced. When she was finished, her fingers didn't leave the strings but instead began another song, this one lively and upbeat.

Dan listened, fascinated with the woman before him. She had survived the blinding snowstorm almost miraculously and brought life and color and music into his quiet existence. And a baby. His gaze dropped to Jane, who looked perfectly content in her makeshift crib. He reached over and turned off the nearby reading lamp, telling himself he'd only darkened the room to allow the baby to sleep. Jessie didn't seem to notice. Her voice rose on the final note, and she let her fingers trail over the strings until the last exquisite drop of sound escaped into the air.

"Beautiful," was the only thing Dan could think to say. "You have a beautiful voice."

She shook her head, her silky blond hair brushing her shoulders. "I wish record producers felt that way."

"They must all be deaf."

Instead of answering, she sang a bittersweet song about two people in love, but destined to remain apart. Then an old folk ballad, and other, older folk songs. Dan began to relax, confident now that Jessie would continue to play and sing in the semidarkness of the warm room. For a few hours anyway, he would not have to be alone. In exchange for sheltering a stranger from a Colorado blizzard, he could pretend his life held warmth and laughter and babies and love.

Not a bad bargain. Not a bad bargain at all.

# 3

HE LISTENED as the music bubbled out of the golden-haired woman on the couch as if a bottle had been uncorked. At one point during the night, Dan poured brandy and put a glass on the scarred pine table in front of Jess, but he didn't think she noticed it. When Jane began to fuss, he opened one of the small cans of formula and filled her bottle. Then he stuck it in a pan of hot water, the way he'd seen Gus do it, until the formula was warm enough for the baby to drink.

He held little Jane and fed her as if he'd done it a thousand times in the middle of dark mountain nights. He fed her and burped her and held her as she fought sleep, and still the music continued, surrounding them with its beauty.

Jessie Carter sang songs he recognized from college, songs from old albums his brother had played so many years ago. Songs disk jockeys played on the radio, only Jessie's distinctive voice and tempo made them more than copies from country's top forty.

And there were the songs he'd never heard before, the ones about traveling and singing and loving. Songs about rejection and pain, grief and loss, triumphant love and true friendship. Funny songs about trucks and bars and being a woman in love. The music flowed through her, songs that rocked and songs that soothed as her fingers moved effortlessly from one melody to the next.

He didn't notice the tears until he replaced the sleeping infant in her bed. Kneeling near Jessie, he heard the catch in her voice and the huskiness of her next words. The silver tears were barely visible in the dim light, but he watched, fascinated, as they slipped down her cheeks.

He tried to listen to the words, but the tears were too distracting. She was a woman alone, traveling to Tennessee in an old truck, and she had a right to her secrets.

"Jessie," he whispered, when the song was over.

"What?" she looked at him as if she had forgotten he was there.

"Are you all right?"

"What?"

"You're crying."

"I am?" She lifted her hand from the neck of the guitar and touched her fingers to her face. "Oh. I guess I am." She attempted a smile. "Must have been a sadder song than I thought."

"Did you write it?"

"Yes."

Maybe there were secrets she needed to tell. "About the man you left?"

She shook her head and propped the guitar against the couch. "About the man who left *me*." She tried to smile. "There's a difference, you see."

"Why?" He leaned over and handed her the brandy glass. She took a sip.

"Why is there a difference?"

"No." He knew all too well the answer to that. Dan joined her on the couch. "Why did he leave you?"

"He said I wasn't 'keeping up.'" She tried to smile. "The one person I thought loved me, and here he was saying I wasn't good enough. And he was right."

Dan took her chin and gently turned her face to his. "That's ridiculous. You're better than anyone I hear on the radio."

"Well, thanks." She gave him a watery smile, and he dropped his hand from her face before she could think he was making a move on her. "But the kicker to the story is that as soon as they—my band—found another singer, they were offered a recording contract and a national tour. Mick was right—I wasn't good enough. Even the song I gave them is just a filler on the album, something for the B side."

"I thought you were heading to Nashville."

"I'd intended to, when I left L.A. I was going to give it one more try," she told him. "On my own this time. But the longer I drive, the more I think it's a stupid plan."

"What else would you do?"

She shrugged, and once again attempted to smile. "That's the problem, lawman. I don't know anything but music."

"Drink your brandy," he ordered. "You need it."

"True." She looked away from him and drained her glass.

He reached over, grasped the neck of the guitar and pulled the instrument toward her. "Play. Unless you don't know any more songs."

Her eyebrows raised and her eyes twinkled with renewed good humor. "Is that a challenge?"

"Yeah." He leaned back, closed his eyes and waited for the music to begin again.

He wasn't disappointed.

Jess played until her fingers grew tired, and only then did she stop. The songs grew quieter and slower, so she would not wake the sleeping child. She sang songs she hadn't thought of in years, songs she'd heard on the radio this morning, songs she'd written in high school.

And the lawman listened. He didn't attempt to sing along, or suggest what she should play. He simply listened, appearing content to listen to whatever she sang. His simple acceptance warmed the deepest, frozen corners of her heart, and she didn't put the guitar down until her sore fingers gave her no choice.

"Thank you," he said.

"You don't have to thank me. I haven't felt like singing for a very long time. But I probably should have stopped hours ago. I'm surprised I didn't put you to sleep."

"I mean it, Jessie. Thank you for a night I will always remember."

"I will, too." She had the strangest urge to lean her head against his shoulder and curl up against his solid body. Instead she sat up. Thoughts like that would only get her in trouble. "It's late."

"And you must be tired."

He started to move away, but she put her hand on his arm to stop him. She wasn't ready to be alone. "Don't go, not yet."

His face showed surprise, and something else Jessie couldn't identify, but he relaxed back into the couch and faced her. "Will you sing again?"

"After I finish my brandy." She reached for the glass and took a sip. "You're a great audience."

"Do you like performing?"

"I prefer writing."

He shook his head. "I can't understand that. With a voice like yours..."

She tilted her head. "What were you going to say?"

"Nothing you haven't heard before," he said, getting to his feet. "It's late," he said unnecessarily. "I'll get some blankets for the couch."

"Dan..." She wanted to tell him that she was glad he'd liked her singing, but he had left the room as if a hundred ghosts were chasing him. When he returned with an armload of blankets, he dumped them beside her on the couch.

"You can take my bed," he muttered. "I'll sleep out here."

"No." There was no way she was going to toss the man out of his own bed. "I'll sleep on the couch. The baby will probably wake up and need me. I don't know if she sleeps through the night or not."

He stared down at her as if he couldn't decide what to do. "I don't think that's a very good idea."

"Why not?" She waited for him to explain. She wanted to take him into her arms and ease the harsh line of his mouth. Dan MacAdams didn't want her pity, that much she knew. But he was lonely, and so was she. Her insides felt so cold she wondered if she would ever thaw, and she knew from the heat radiating from the wood stove that the chill wasn't physical.

He was in front of her with two swift steps. He lifted her chin and briefly touched his lips to hers. The barest of smiles crossed his face. "Don't look at me like that. I brought you here to be safe, not to be seduced." He took her shoulders, turned her in the direction of the bedroom and gave her a little push. "I'll take care of the child. You don't have to worry about her. Go."

Jess went. She walked through the doorway and

closed the heavy pine door behind her. A plump bed-side lamp illuminated the small room. A pile of clothes lay in a corner, probably the former contents of Jane's bed. Jessie's pillow and tote bag sat atop a bright quilt in the middle of the double bed, and an open door revealed a tiny bathroom with a shower stall in the corner. There were clean towels stacked on a shelf above the toilet, and Jess couldn't resist the chance to take a hot shower. Maybe if she stood under a stream of hot water she wouldn't feel so damn cold and lonely. Maybe then she wouldn't long for a stranger's warmth to surround her, a stranger's arms to shelter her from the howling wind.

She heard the baby's cries when she turned off the shower. She dried off quickly, tossed her flannel nightgown over her head and hurried out to the living room.

Dan held the red-faced baby in his arms, a distraught expression on his face. Jess held out her arms, and Dan handed her the screaming child. He'd removed his sweater; the dark shirt underneath was unbuttoned, revealing a V-neck T-shirt hugging a very wide male chest.

Jess turned her attention back to the sobbing baby. "What's wrong?"

"I don't know. All of a sudden she woke up screaming. I tried to feed her, but she just got mad."

Jess tucked the baby against her shoulder and patted her back. "She shouldn't be hungry. Didn't you feed her a couple of hours ago?"

"Yeah." He ran his hands through his hair. "While you were singing."

"Did you change her diaper?"

"Uh, no."

Jess took the baby over to the couch. "That must be the problem. She has a little diaper rash, I think, and hates being wet."

He waited as she exchanged the sopping wet disposable diaper for a dry one, then tucked the T-shirt around her. Jane's cries turned to hiccups, then subsided into a small sigh. "I'm starting to get to know this little lady," Jess declared.

"That was it?" He walked over to the couch and looked down at the child. "All that was over wet pants?"

"I guess so." Jessie scooped her into her arms and set her back into the drawer. "There, you fussy thing, go back to sleep."

"She scared me to death," he admitted. "I thought she was dying."

Jess tucked the blanket around her. "I was scared, too. I'll sit here until she falls asleep."

"Good idea." He moved to the kitchen and picked up his glass. "I'm going to have another drink. Do you want anything?"

She kept her voice low. "What you're having, thanks."

He brought her brandy and sat down on the floor beside her. "To dry pants," he said, touching his glass to hers.

"To dry pants," she echoed, smiling up at him. "Let's hope these last awhile."

He shuddered. "I don't think I want to go through that again."

"You don't have children?"

"No."

"That's what I thought. I figure you for a confirmed bachelor."

"And you'd be right."

"You obviously like living alone, then."

"No." His voice was flat. "I hate it."

"Then why aren't you married? With a wife and six kids to keep you company?"

"Things don't always work out the way you want them to, Jessie." He put his glass down beside him and grasped her shoulders. "Hell. I told myself I wouldn't do this."

He eyed her mouth, and his face dipped closer to hers. "Do it anyway," she whispered, and his lips took hers in a searing kiss.

Jess kissed him back, promising herself tomorrow she would get into the truck and drive away...alone. This night would be a memory she would always treasure, a night with a stranger and a baby. Tonight might be the closest she'd ever come to domesticity and motherhood. There was no room for husbands and children on the road.

He lifted his mouth from hers, his eyes dark in the dim light.

"I've been alone for a long time," he warned. "I haven't wanted to be with anyone, not until now."

She stood up and faced him. "I don't want to be alone, either," she confessed. Was she crazy to do this? She'd never in her life been this attracted to a stranger.

"I don't know what will come of th—"

She put her finger on his lips. "Shh."

Dan moved closer and pulled her into his arms. Jessie Carter went, willingly. Telling herself that holding him couldn't hurt, promising herself that whatever happened tonight wouldn't matter tomorrow. Because it was a magical night, the two of them brought together to make love to each other and ease the empty places in their hearts, at least for a little while. At least for one night.

The wind blew a fierce curtain of snow against the window, making Jess jump. Dan held her tightly. "I don't like storms," she whispered.

"I do. This one brought you to me," he explained, dipping his head lower. Once again he took her lips with a tenderness Jess hadn't known was possible in a kiss. He released her after long moments, stood up and took her hand, and lifted her from the floor.

Jessie hesitated, looking down at the baby. "Jane—"

"Is asleep," Dan whispered. "We'll leave the door open so we can hear her if she wakes up." He chuckled. "She doesn't have any trouble making herself heard."

Jess gripped his fingers and turned to gaze up at him. "Tell me I'm not crazy."

He shook his head. "I think we both are."

That made her smile. "If I were crazy I wouldn't be so nervous."

"Come to bed, Jessie Carter," he whispered, moving toward the bedroom door. "Neither of us is going to be alone tonight."

His touch was warm, his fingers gentle around hers until he released her hand to fix the bed. He moved her things to the floor, pushed back the quilt and gestured toward the wide mattress.

She climbed in and tucked her nightgown carefully around her bare legs. When Dan switched off the lamp the only light in the cozy darkness was a faint glow from the kitchen area around the corner. Jess pulled the covers over her lap and watched in quiet fascination as Dan removed his shirt and tugged the T-shirt over his head. Both dropped onto the floor, but Dan didn't seem to notice. He quickly removed the rest of his clothing. Jess caught a glimpse of muscled thighs and furred chest before he climbed into the other side of the bed and hauled the quilts to his waist to cover his nakedness.

She turned to face him. His eyes were shadowed, but she knew there was nothing to fear from this man. Nothing except the trembling that began within her as he reached to take her in his arms. She moved her hands along his neck; he was warm and strong under her fingertips. His heart pounding against her breast as he took her mouth and parted her lips with his tongue until he possessed her completely.

She smoothed her palms along his shoulders. His hands bunched the folds of her nightgown at her waist.

Dan lifted his lips from hers and gazed down into her gray eyes. He hadn't expected the passion. Lust, yes, he'd felt that, almost since the first moment he saw her. That honey hair and velvet voice had entranced him.

Her songs had seduced him.

And the heat from her skin was hotter than burning cedar.

He lifted her gown; she helped him ease it over her head. He flung it to the floor, and her golden hair tumbled against her bare shoulders.

Dan's breath caught in his throat. The woman was so beautiful. Her breasts were small, perfect and full, her waist curved, her skin glowed like satin. He smoothed his fingers down her breast to touch one delicate nipple, and she shivered. "You're cold," he said. "Get under the covers."

She slipped down, and he followed her. They lay on their sides, facing each other, but Dan didn't want to rush. He wanted to make each minute last an hour, so the night would never end. He moved the sheet to cover her bare shoulder and his fingers lingered at her neck, and pulled her to him. He kissed her and her arms went around his neck.

With his hand he swept lower, to skim her waist and hips under the heavy warmth of the quilts. He tugged her warm body close to him, reveling in the feeling of skin to skin contact. She was heat and silk and softness, she was what he dreamed of at night when the wind howled down the mountain and darkness surrounded the cabin. Desire, hot and heavy, outweighed his intentions to go slowly, and her hands on his shoulders and her lips underneath his threatened to push him over the edge of control.

He pushed her onto her back; she murmured her approval.

He wanted to touch every inch of her sweet skin, wanted to feel her under his lips. Her fingers pressed into his back, urging him closer.

He paused. He had to taste her first. He trailed kisses along her breasts, pausing to lave each nipple, listening to the sweet whimpers from the woman beneath him. He moved lower, to kiss the smooth skin of her abdomen, to tangle his fingers in the curly V between her legs. He stroked the soft folds, felt the slick wetness touch his fingers, caressed the sensitive nub with his thumb until she moaned aloud.

There would be no more waiting, except to slip on a condom. He returned to the warmth of her body and slid over her.

He paused. Jess looked up into his eyes, forgetting he had been a stranger until a few hours ago. She tried to smile, and he bent his head and kissed a corner of her mouth.

"Afraid?"

She shook her head. "I should be, but I'm not."

"I won't hurt you," he promised, his voice low.

And Jessie believed him. She held his hips, he pushed her thighs apart with his knee. He slid himself inside of her in a slow, sweetly torturous motion. The crinkly hair on his chest brushed against her breasts, and his legs kept her thighs apart, allowing him entrance. Her fingers gripped his buttocks, urging him closer. He moved deeper still, and the sensation sent shocks throughout her body. He partially withdrew, then thrust deep; he was hot and hard inside of her, his motions controlled as he moved within her.

Hours or minutes passed, Jess didn't know, didn't care, as they made love to each other under the covers of the warm bed. They moved to their sides, still joined in a heated madness that continued as he rolled onto his back and she sprawled on top of him. He grasped her buttocks, she smoothed his hair from his forehead. He moved within her again and again, as if he knew this would be the only time they would ever be together, as if he would need this memory to burn throughout the coming long winter. And when she was on her back again, and he moved faster within her, they came together with a shattering explosion of senses. Jess clung to his waist until she caught her breath, until she remembered her name, until she remembered where she lay.

Dan's breathing slowed, but his heart pounded against her breast for long moments. He rolled from her, but stayed close, then tucked her against the solid warmth of his body and made certain she was covered by the quilts. "Close your eyes, Jessie Carter. We'll pretend we hold each other every night, that you warm your feet on my legs and complain about my snoring."

She nestled into him, surprisingly relaxed. She would have thought she would feel awkward now, but there was an easy intimacy between them. "Do you snore?"

"You tell me, in the morning."

But they were awake long before dawn rose from behind the mountain. Jess heard the baby's cries and eased from Dan's sleepy embrace to find her nightgown. She fed and changed the child, held her in the recliner and sang a soft lullaby until Jane's eyes closed once again. Dan came into the living room, wearing jeans and nothing else.

"Is everything all right?"

"Fine," Jessie whispered. "I'll be back to bed in a minute."

"I'll wait for you," he said. He opened the stove and added two more logs, shut the door and adjusted the draft. Then he went over to the window and pulled back the curtains. "I think the worst of the storm is over."

Jess tucked the sleeping child into her bed, then walked over to Dan. She moved the curtain back into place, effectively shutting out the night. "Come back to bed."

"Gladly." He held her, resting his chin on the top of her head. He smoothed the flannel gown along her hips. "Take this damn thing off," he growled.

Jessie laughed and let him tug her into the bedroom. Naked once again, they held each other under the warmth of the quilts. She snuggled against him, her head on his shoulder.

"I still don't know anything about you," she said, touching the hair on his chest.

"Maybe there isn't much to know."

"Was there ever a Mrs. Lawman?"

"Jess, I don't—"

"Was there?" she interrupted.

He sighed. "Yes, fortunately. Once."

"And?" she prompted.

"She died last year. Cancer."

That was not what Jess had expected to hear, and the bleak expression in Dan's eyes made her chest ache. "I'm so sorry."

"By the time she died, I thought I was prepared for it. She'd...suffered." He paused, looking past Jessie's shoulder to a bare spot on the wall. When he looked down at Jessie again, his expression was carefully controlled. "But I'm still not used to spending these damn winter nights alone."

"Then I'm glad I could keep you company," she managed to say. She reached out her hand and he took it, and held it snugly against his chest. "Tell me about her," she asked. "What was her name?"

He hesitated for a fraction of a second, then smiled the saddest smile she'd ever seen. "All right. If you want. Her name was Carol."

Jess listened as he told her how they'd played together as children, how they'd grown up together. The prom, graduation and marriage during college. About buying land on the mountain and building a house made of logs and glass, with a view of the valley that would take his breath away each morning. He talked of the law-enforcement academy and Carol's teaching job, of their plans to have children and teach them to ski. He spoke of her illness, her pain and her courage, and her funeral. And about selling the house and moving to the other side of the mountain.

While he talked Jess held his hand and listened, hearing the undercurrent of pain in every word he spoke. He spoke of love and devotion and dying, while she had been feeling sorry for herself for being dumped by a selfish guitar player with an ego the size of Minnesota.

"You shouldn't be alone," she whispered. "It's not right."

"Right or not, it's the way it is." He moved over her. "Except for tonight." He lowered his mouth to her breast and caressed the nipple with his lips. He took his time, moving along her skin with his hands and his lips. His tongue touched the places of Jessie's body that his fingers had explored before. He kissed and caressed with gentle intimacy until Jessie cried out in release, then he covered her with his body and entered her once again. He was slow and certain, learning what she liked and how she liked it, until passion took him over the edge and sent him gasping for breath.

They clung to each other in the darkness, and finally slept.

"YOU SURE you don't want anything to eat?"

"I'm sure." Jessie dropped the tote bag by the kitchen door, then plopped her pillow on top of it. "I'm not much of a breakfast person."

He motioned toward a pottery mug on the round table. "I poured you some coffee."

"Thanks." Jess sat down reluctantly across from him. She didn't want to have to make small talk, didn't want to prolong leaving him and leaving Jane. This was harder than she'd imagined it could be, and she was tired of goodbyes.

Especially the kind that gripped her heart and squeezed until the tears rose behind her eyes. She took a sip and looked at the man seated across from her. He was freshly shaven, but pale. He wore a khaki uniform and a badge, and looked so official and remote that she wanted to cry. The man who had made love to her last night didn't exist this morning. At least, she couldn't see him.

"What's going to happen to Jane?" she managed to ask.

"I've talked to a few people this morning. She'll be put in a foster home until the authorities can find her mother."

A miserable feeling overcame her. "And if they can't?"

"I imagine parental rights will be terminated and she will be adopted."

"By someone nice?"

He nodded. "I'll watch out for her. You have my word on that."

"Thank you." Jess swallowed, trying to ignore the lump in her throat. It was as if she were talking to a stranger. His eyes were cold, his expression polite but distant. Was this the same man who had made love to her with his lips and tongue and body?

Dan stood up and tossed the rest of his coffee in the sink and set his mug on the counter. He kept his back to her while he spoke. "I checked with the state police. The roads are plowed. Go slow and you should be all right."

Well, she could take a hint. She pushed her coffee cup away and walked toward the baby, still tucked safely in her padded drawer. The little girl waved her arms and kicked as she watched Jessie approach. Jess knelt beside her, and gave her a finger to grab on to. "'Bye, sweetheart. You were good company, and I'll miss you." The child gurgled and a smile lifted her tiny lips. "Maybe I'll write a song, just for you. Listen to the radio and maybe one of these days you'll hear me singing to you."

Jess straightened and walked away before she scooped up the child and burst into tears. It was time to leave and, judging from the set face on the man waiting by the door he couldn't wait to open it and get rid of her.

"I put your guitars and blankets in your truck while you were in the shower."

"Thanks." She put on her jacket, collected her belongings and hesitated by the door. Dan's hand gripped the doorknob, but he didn't pull the door open. He looked down at her for a long moment, then reached out to cup the back of her neck. He pulled her toward him for a short, harsh kiss before releasing her.

"Don't look back," he growled, and opened the door. Jess, her knees shaking, stepped outside onto a narrow strip of bare ground. He'd been so anxious to get rid of her he'd shovelled a path straight to the parking lot.

She blinked against the blinding glare of the sun on the snow, and turned to catch one last look at him in the doorway. But the door closed, ending any second thoughts she might have had about leaving. Besides, she told herself, as she negotiated the slippery path, she was on her way to Nashville. To be rich and famous. Successful and...alone.

She choked back the tears, loaded the truck and

hopped behind the wheel. Resisting the urge to catch a final glimpse of the cabin, Jess guided the truck out of the freshly plowed parking lot and headed down the road.

There was no reason to stay in Colorado.

DAN DIDN'T TURN AWAY from the window until Jessie had disappeared from sight. The baby in his arms squirmed, trying to touch his chin with her pudgy fingers. "Well, that's that," he told her. "She's gone."

He left the window and went back to the living room. He sat on the couch and cradled Jane in his arms. The cabin was depressing, empty and quiet except for the snapping of the logs burning in the stove. The baby watched him, her eyes wide.

Dan tried to smile at her, but his face seemed frozen. "Some things are just too good to last, I guess." He gave the baby his thumb to hold. Her touch was oddly comforting. "Don't worry, sweetheart," he managed, his voice husky, "no matter what happens, I'll make sure that you'll be safe."

# 4

"JESSIE, THIS IS CRAZY. Tell me you're not goin' to do this."

"No." Jessie tossed an extra pair of jeans in the overflowing suitcase and ignored Billy's pacing. "I'm not going to tell you any such thing. I'm...tired. The tour is over and I'm not getting back on this bus again 'til next year." She dropped the lid over the clothes and struggled to zip the suitcase shut.

"I don't know why you can't rest in Nashville," he grumbled, shoving a sequined dress out of the way so he could sit on the bed. "Just 'cause you're a little dragged out doesn't mean you have to get off the bus in the middle of nowhere. Why don't you come back home with the rest of us?"

Jess pulled the suitcase onto the narrow passageway between her bed and her makeup table. "Because you'd have me working, that's why."

He didn't argue with that statement, Jess noticed.

"At least tell me where you're going," Billy pleaded. "Just in case I need to get in touch with you."

"So you can badger me about business? No way." She pulled a sweatshirt over her head and swept her hair back in a ponytail. "We've had a hundred meetings in the past weeks. Everything's taken care of." She hung her purse over her shoulder, grabbed her old guitar case and began to kick the suitcase down the aisle toward the front of the bus.

"I'll get that." Billy sighed and brushed past her to pick up the suitcase. "Since you're so damn determined to get out of here."

"I haven't had a vacation in over three years," Jess grumbled. "And you're trying to make me feel guilty."

"I'm just trying to make you come to your senses. I wouldn't be a good manager if I didn't try."

Jess climbed down from the bus and surveyed the parking lot of the Holiday Inn. The Jeep she'd leased was parked nearby, a shiny, white, four-wheel-drive vehicle that would take her far away from the bus she'd lived on for nine months. In the far distance, dark mountains rose from the plains. A dust-filled gust of wind made her blink. "What town are we in?"

"Casper."

"Wyoming?"

"Yeah." He gestured toward the suitcase. "What do you want me to do with this?"

"Put it in the Jeep, Billy." She followed him to her getaway car, as she thought of it, and tossed her old guitar on the back seat. Before she opened the car door, she stopped and hugged him. He frowned at her and at the car. "And thanks."

"At least call me when you get settled," Billy grumbled. "So I know my favorite singer is safe."

"I will. Promise." She slid behind the wheel of the car, switched on the engine and pressed a button to lower the window. "Don't worry about me, Billy. I'll come back with a suitcase full of new songs."

He grinned. "You'd better, darlin'. You owe Peach Tree Records a new album by spring, and then we launch the summer tour."

"You don't have to remind me." The very thought gave her nightmares. She fastened her seat belt and waved goodbye, then backed the Jeep out of the parking space. Within minutes she was on Interstate 25, heading south.

To Colorado.

Jess turned on the radio and pushed the buttons until she found a clear station. "And now," the disk jockey drawled, "I'm gonna play you all a song you're sure to remember. Three years ago a lovely lady burst upon the country scene with this song, 'Colorado Snow.' It broke our hearts, it did, and we all fell in love with...Jessie Carter."

Jess turned off the radio before the guitar played three notes of the opening bar. Now *there* was timing for you. "Colorado Snow" had made her a bunch of money, had even made her famous. It had been her first big break, her first hit song, but it still embarrassed her to hear herself on the radio.

Besides, she thought, feeling the familiar tension hit the pit of her stomach, she didn't know if she would ever be able to write another song.

"COME ON, ANNA. Daddy has to go to work." He looked up at the clock on the bureau. *And Daddy's late. Again.*

"'Kay." The little girl picked up her stuffed dog. "We're ready."

Dan knelt down and zipped her yellow jacket. "It's getting cold out."

"Miss Jones says winter's coming. We're making Hall'ween stuff next week."

"That's good." He opened the door and ushered her into the carpeted hall. The corridor was quiet in the section of the hotel that served as their private apartment. They slipped down the back staircase, avoided the clamor of the kitchen and hurried outside to the boardwalk. Sunshine brightened the wood exteriors of the old buildings that lined Main Street, but the breeze was cool, a reminder that winter was coming fast.

"I'm gonna be a princess. Or a monster."

"Fine," Dan agreed, taking her hand in his as they crossed the street. They walked the two blocks down the hill to the preschool, and up the steps of the bright blue house.

"It's sharing day today," Anna stated happily.

Dan opened the door and paused. "Give me a kiss," he said, bending down to smile into her round face. Her gray eyes sparkled at him and she kissed him on the nose, then giggled as he crossed his eyes.

"'Bye, Daddy."

"See you tonight," he called after her as she scampered inside to join her classmates and their incredibly patient teacher.

Dan turned away and went back down the steps. It was a steep walk up the hill to the main part of town. The Gold Bar Hotel stood between the Opera House and the Outlaw Saloon in the highest part of Gold City. The road looped around the top of the hill and down the other side, covering a little over a mile before it ended back where it had started in the lower end of town. Only one road led out of Gold City, a well-maintained one that wound down the mountain for over twenty miles before bumping into the interstate that intersected Colorado from east to west.

Denver was less than two hours away, if the roads were clear, but he didn't go there often. There was no reason to.

He looked up at the mountains that would soon be snow-covered. It was October already...again. The years kept flying by. Anna was four now, growing up fast. Pretty soon she'd be asking questions he didn't want to answer. Questions about her birth mother and a country-western singer.

Maybe he'd play "Colorado Snow" on the CD player and try to explain something he didn't understand himself. Dan shrugged off his worry, wondering why he felt so unsettled this morning. Maybe they were about to get a storm. Dan lengthened his stride and hurried toward the top of the hill and a fresh cup of coffee. With luck, Maizie would have saved him a cinnamon roll.

THE DINER SAT EMPTY, its front windows boarded up. A bright red For Lease sign hung on the front door. Jess parked the Jeep in the empty parking lot and shut off the engine. She stared at the diner for a long moment before getting out of the car. Maybe Dan still lived in back. Maybe the cook did, too.

She followed the narrow gravel path around to the back of the building. The cabin was just as she remembered, except for the weeds that surrounded it. White with snow before, now it seemed dark and forlorn.

She peeked in the window. The room was empty, except for the rug on the floor. Well, she thought, shivering in the cool air, that was that. Dan MacAdams was gone to Lord knew where, and little baby Jane must have a new family and a new name. She blinked back tears on the way back to the car. What had she expected, anyway? That Dan would be waiting by the door to greet her?

It was a silly dream. All of it, just a silly dream.

She got back in the car and examined the maps she'd picked up in Denver. She flipped through the brochures, hoping something would appeal to her. She didn't want to get caught up in these mountains at night again.

*Gold City. Relive Gold Rush days in one of Colorado's most authentic mining towns. Stay at the Gold Bar Hotel, gamble in the many saloons on Main Street, experience the excitement of the Old West.*

Jess had always wanted to see a town like that. The colored photos made it look as if Billy the Kid might walk down the street. And the simple map showed that she was close enough to spend the night. If she could find the right road, of course. She'd debated about staying in Denver, but she was tired of cities. She wanted something different, somewhere off the beaten track, at least for tonight.

Jess turned away from the diner, trying to ignore the disappointment of not finding Dan MacAdams, and drove the Jeep out of the gravel lot. Suddenly she was very, very tired.

THE DAY HADN'T BEEN much different than any other, thank God. The hotel was less than half full, typical for October. Later on, during ski season, it would fill up on weekends, but Dan could wait. He didn't mind a slow spell every once in awhile. Gave him a chance to catch up on paperwork and clean up the office.

He pushed a stack of papers to the right-hand corner of the large oak desk. The dark-panelled room needed dusting. He'd inherited this room, just as he'd inherited the hotel. His brother Wade's hunting prints hung on the wall behind the desk; Wade and Susie's wedding picture stood in an ornate frame on top of the wooden file cabinet. Tucked behind the reception area, the windowless office's only door faced the reception desk and the wide doors of the entrance. Dan stood and looked at his watch. He would have to hurry if he was going to be on time to pick up Anna.

"You calling it quits for the day?" Grace looked up as he entered the reception area.

"It's five o'clock already."

"Did you have a chance to go over the estimates for the new heating system?"

"Yes. I'd do it, if I thought there'd be enough business in the winter to justify it."

The older woman chuckled. "You said that last year."

Dan peered into the lobby. Two couples sat talking on the Victorian love seats, and the clink of glassware came from beyond, in the bar. He'd opted to limit gambling to three small slot machines in the back of the saloon, thinking his customers would appreciate a quiet haven from the noisy gambling machines that filled many of the saloons on Main Street. "Looks quiet enough. Anything I should know about?"

"We've had two arrivals, one with reservations, one without. The Porters decided to stay an extra day. Mary fixed the vacuum cleaner, and Marc's serving trout tonight."

"Anna likes that."

"Anna likes *everything*," Grace pointed out. "That child sure can eat!"

"I'm going to go get her." He stepped into the foyer and peeked into the dining room. The edgy feeling he'd woken with grew stronger. He turned back to Grace. "Are you sure nothing's wrong?"

"Not that I know of," she replied. "Why?"

He shrugged. "I don't know. Just a strange feeling, I guess."

"Maybe you need a vacation."

"I'm not tired, just edgy." He headed toward the wide double doors and grasped one of the brass door-knobs beneath etched-glass panels. He turned back to Grace before opening the door. "Are we supposed to get a storm tonight?"

"No. I heard the weather report twenty minutes ago." She waved him away. "Quit worrying and go get that child."

"Any message for Beth?"

"No. Just tell me how she looks. This pregnancy is awfully hard on her."

"All right." Dan went outside and took a deep breath of fresh air. The setting sun was sending shadows down from the hills. There was a chill in the air, but so far no sign of bad weather. He headed toward the other side of town to pick up Anna at Beth's house. He didn't know what he'd do without Grace's daughter. She picked up Anna at preschool each day and took her home for the afternoon. She was happy with the extra money she earned baby-sitting, and Dan needed to get in a full day's work. The combined duties of hotel owner and local sheriff took up a lot of hours, even with extra help.

Dan quickened his pace, anxious to see Anna and know that she was all right. They would return to the hotel and have dinner in the dining room, just like they did every night. Later he would tuck her into bed with her stuffed animals and wait by her side until she fell asleep. There was no reason to feel apprehensive. It was just another Monday.

"NO ROOM SERVICE?" Jess echoed. She held the phone closer to her ear, wondering if she'd heard correctly. "Really?"

"Really," the woman replied. "The dining room is open from five until nine p.m. for dinner. And every morning, from six to ten, a breakfast buffet is served. Lunch is from eleven-thirty until two, and we can fix you a box lunch if you're going on a hike, but there is no room service."

"I'm not exactly dressed for anything fancy."

The woman chuckled. "Anything goes here in Gold City, believe me. We draw the line at bathing suits and bare chests, but otherwise I wouldn't worry about it, if I were you."

"Well, thank you for the information."

"You're welcome. If there's anything else I can do for you, please let me know."

Jess replaced the receiver in its cradle and leaned back against the headboard. The Gold Bar Hotel was exactly as she'd pictured, except larger. Her room was on the third floor, near the wide red-carpeted staircase. The blue-and-white room was papered in a tiny floral print; the carpet was a dark gold. The double bed sat between tall windows covered in gold damask and faced a mahogany dresser. An armoire contained a small television and several wide drawers, and a bedside table held a radio, a telephone and an ornate lamp. Jess had peeked into the bathroom, admired the deep claw-footed tub, and hung her few clothes in the closet near the door.

She wanted to stay in this bed for the next week. Instead, she had to wash up and go down to the dining room and have dinner by herself.

She hated eating alone. It was right up there with going to the dentist and using the bathroom in a gas station. Besides, with all the guys in the crew and the band, she'd rarely had to worry about eating alone. Lots of times they'd just ordered something to go and ate on the bus. There were usually too many miles to cover.

Jess moved slowly off the bed and eyed her rumpled jeans. She slipped her loafers back on, picked up her brass key and headed for the door. Her stomach growled in anticipation as she hurried down the wide staircase.

A huge crystal chandelier hung over the lobby and she could hear conversation and the tinkling of glasses coming from the bar. All she needed was a red satin dress and she could burst into a bawdy song to entertain the cowboys. She nodded to the gray-haired woman behind the desk and crossed the lobby to the dining room. There didn't seem to be anyone to seat her, so she looked around the large room for a small, inconspicuous table.

The tables were covered with white linen and sparkling silverware; only a few held people. The room was fancier than she'd thought it would be, but the other diners wore casual clothes, so Jess started to relax. If she could find a quiet table, she'd eat her dinner and hurry back to that soft bed as soon as possible.

A man seated near the far corner turned around to wave at the waitress and Jessie saw Dan MacAdams. She blinked, wondering if she'd deceived herself into seeing what she'd wanted to see all along.

She started toward him, then hesitated. Was this man really the lawman who'd come to her rescue years before? His dark hair was longer and there were a few more lines around his eyes and mouth, but the face was the same, the shoulders still impressively wide. He smiled as the young waitress approached, the heart-stopping smile Jessie remembered from their night together.

Jess took a seat near him. His food hadn't arrived, she noted, so he wasn't going to be leaving right away. She needed time to calm the nervous fluttering in her stomach, to prepare something to say to him.

And there was a child, too, she noticed. He was married, then. Disappointment was sharp and fierce, but Jess didn't question why that realization hurt. The child was tiny; Jess guessed the little blond girl was not yet four. It was highly unlikely that Dan would still have Jane. No one would have given custody of an infant to a widowed sheriff's deputy.

The child could be his niece. Or a friend's child.

"Good evening," the waitress said. She was young, with brown hair tied back in a ponytail, and she wore a white blouse and black slacks. She gave Jessie a menu and blocked her view of Dan MacAdams and the little girl. "Our special tonight is trout, baked or fried with your choice of rice pilaf or a baked potato. The vegetable is acorn squash. That's ten-ninety-five and includes coffee or tea."

"Thank you, but I think I'll pass on the fish."

"Well, the roast beef is good. And the chicken florentine is really popular." The girl tipped her head. "Have you been here before? You look familiar."

"No. This is my first time in Gold City."

The waitress looked disappointed. "Oh. You look like someone I've seen before. Would you like anything to drink before your dinner?"

Jessie opened her menu and noted the simple choices. "A glass of white wine, please."

"Sure." The waitress was gone at last and Jessie could see Dan's table. He wore a blue sweater, with a white collar showing above it, and dark gray slacks. The little girl giggled at something he said, then chattered to the waitress as she delivered their dinner.

Jess tried not to stare at them too much. She was nervous. What was she going to say to him: "Remember me? The stranger you slept with one night four years ago?"

The young waitress came back to the table and took a pencil and pad from her pocket. "Have you decided what you'll have this evening?" She blocked Jess's view of Dan.

"The special is fine," Jess murmured.

The girl looked surprised. Jess wished she'd move. "The fish?"

"Whatever."

"Baked or fried? With rice or baked potato?"

"Surprise me." *Just move to the right about six inches.*

Maybe he wouldn't remember her, she worried. But who could forget a night with an abandoned baby and a freak October snowstorm? She'd never forgotten. Which was why she was in this part of Colorado, to search for a man she'd only known for fifteen hours, but who had changed her life forever.

Dan ordered dessert. Jess ate her fish and drank her wine and ordered another glass. She would talk to him before he left the dining room, she decided. He might be travelling through town, even if Gold City was in the middle of nowhere. But she thought she heard the waitress call him by name. And the child seemed comfortable in the restaurant, as if she was accustomed to eating out.

He lingered over coffee while the little girl played with a dish of ice cream.

Jess pushed her plate away and waved to the waitress, who hurried over. "Was everything all right?"

"Just fine. Can I put this on my bill here at the hotel?"

"You're a guest?"

"Yes."

"No problem." She handed her the bill. "Just put your name and room number on here."

Jess added a generous tip and signed her name, then handed the paper back to the girl. "Thanks."

Dan stood and pushed his chair away from the table. The little girl hopped off her chair and noticed Jessie watching her. She smiled, and Jess smiled back. Dan turned, following the child's gaze, and froze as his gaze met Jessie's.

Jessie stood, her knees shaking. Did he remember her? She couldn't tell. He turned away, tossed his napkin on the table, and said something to the little girl that made her look up at him with wide eyes as Jess approached the table.

"Dan?"

His frown deepened the lines around his mouth. "Yes?"

Jess felt her stomach drop to her feet. "You don't remember me."

"Should I?" His voice was cold.

Jess faltered. "I guess not."

"Daddy?" The child tugged on her father's hand. He wasn't wearing a wedding ring, Jess noticed, but now she knew the little girl belonged to him. Where was Mrs. MacAdams? Probably working late.

"Just a minute," he told her, then turned back to Jessie. "I'm sorry," he said, but he didn't sound the least bit apologetic. "You'll have to excuse us."

Jess backed away, and Dan guided the child around her and out of the dining room. Jess returned to her table to collect her leather purse. She wanted to go up to her private little room and pull the covers over her head so no one would hear her cry.

Four years ago Dan MacAdams had made her feel loved. He'd appreciated her music, he'd comforted her in the long hours of the storm. He'd made her feel that her songs were important. And then he'd forgotten her.

"GRACE, IS THERE a Jessie Carter registered here?"

Grace checked the guest registry. "There sure is. Room 315."

Dan swore under his breath, then turned the book toward him so he could see for himself. Her scrawled signature filled the third line from the top of the page.

"I think she's some sort of country singer," Grace added. "She looked familiar, and the name is, too. I might've seen her picture on Beth's CDs."

Dan replaced the ledger. Yes, Jessie's picture was on the cover of her CDs. He should know; he had all four of them sitting on a shelf in his room.

"Isn't that something, having a famous singer staying here in Gold City. What do you think she's doing here?"

He'd like to know the answer to that question, too. "I wouldn't know, Grace. Maybe she's a tourist, just like everyone else."

"I suppose. Did you put Anna to bed?"

He nodded. "She went right to sleep."

Grace turned back to her computer. "I'm almost done entering the figures for September."

Dan drummed a pencil on the counter and surveyed the empty lobby. There was a burst of laughter from the bar. "I'm going to call it a night," he muttered. "Tell Jeff to call if he needs me."

"All right. He's still in his room, but I'll call him down when I'm ready to leave."

Dan barely heard her. He took the back staircase to the third floor, checked on Anna to make sure she was still sleeping, then made his way to the guest corridor. The door to room 315 opened and Dan caught a glimpse of blond hair and dark blue T-shirt as she peered out.

He put his hand on the door, pushed it open and stepped inside. "What are you doing here, Jessie?"

Jessie stared up at him. "You remembered."

"Yes." She looked the same, except thinner. Too thin, he noted, as she stepped back to pick up her robe from the rumpled bed. Dark shadows smudged the skin under her eyes, and he swallowed the wave of concern that washed over him. Jessie Carter's health was none of his business.

She shrugged on the pink robe and gestured toward the desk chair. "Have a seat, lawman."

"How did you find me?"

Jessie perched on the edge of the bed and pulled the edges of her robe over her breasts. "Actually, it was an accident. I'm on vacation and ended up here. I never expected to run into you in a hotel."

He didn't believe her. "I own this place," he said.

Her eyebrows rose. "That's quite a career change."

"There have been a lot of changes in the past four years."

"I see that. You remarried, you have a daughter. Congratulations."

"Thank you." He leaned against the door and crossed his arms in front of his chest. "What's a famous country singer doing in Gold City?"

"I'm on vacation. Why did you pretend you didn't know me downstairs?"

"I wasn't sure it was you. Not until I checked the guest registry," he lied. He didn't want her to know that seeing her again had shaken him up so badly he didn't know what else to do but to deny knowing her. He didn't want her to know who Anna was. "Why did you pick Gold City for a vacation?"

"I didn't really, not at first. Could you sit down? You're making me nervous standing there like that, as if I'm on trial or something."

He sat.

"I've wanted to come back to Colorado for a long time," she continued, more relaxed now that he was at eye level. "I always wondered what happened to the baby, what happened to you." She leaned forward. "Did you ever find her mother?"

"The hitchhiker? No. No one knew anything about her."

"Did you find a home for little Jane?"

Dan kept his voice even. "She was put in foster care, and later adopted."

Jessie smiled. "Thank goodness. I'm glad that worked out. I've thought about her so often."

"And you?" He hurried to change the subject. "You obviously made it to Nashville."

"Yes."

"And became a star."

"A very little star," Jess corrected.

He didn't want to be attracted to her, didn't want to find her so appealing sitting on the bed, her hair like silk on the shoulders of the fuzzy pink robe. He told himself he didn't care what had happened between them four years ago.

He lied.

"Have you ever heard my songs?" She seemed almost embarrassed to ask.

"Yes. I always thought you were very...talented. Your albums prove it."

"Thank you." They stared at each other, and the blush on Jessie's cheeks told him she remembered their evening together as well as he did.

Dan stood, anxious to leave before he did something stupid, like take her in his arms. "How long are you staying?"

She stood, too, but didn't move toward the door. "I don't know. Maybe I'll leave in the morning."

Dan nodded. "Well, in that case, I hope you have an enjoyable vacation." He opened the door and turned back to face the woman who had plagued his thoughts for four years. "I'm glad it all worked out the way you wanted it to, Jess."

"Me, too," she said softly.

He turned away from her without saying goodbye and went into the hallway and shut the door behind him. He heard Jess turn the key in the lock a moment later, and he moved quickly toward his own rooms. But his worries stayed with him, long after he checked on Anna and readied himself for bed. The mystery of the hitchhiker had never been solved; in the past few years he'd come to believe that Jessie might have been her real mother, that she'd left her because she had no room for a child in her ambitious plans for herself.

If that were true, was she back to claim her child? He could only pray she would leave in the morning before she saw Anna again. He wouldn't breathe easily until Jessie Carter disappeared from his life again.

Hopefully, for the last time.

# 5

"WANT A REFILL on that coffee, miss?"

Jess pushed her cup across the counter. "Thanks."

"Sure." The waitress moved along the counter, re-filling coffee cups as she went along. The small coffee shop was crowded at this hour of the morning, but Jess was content in the familiar noisy atmosphere. Hotel dining rooms were fine for dinner, but a little formal for a stack of pancakes and a side order of bacon.

Besides, she could listen to people talk while she ate. And sitting at the counter was preferable to sitting alone at a table. After breakfast she'd promised herself a walk around the Main Street of Gold City before she left. The names of the shops and saloons were intriguing: Molly Malone's, The Gold Digger, Last Stop Saloon, and the Gold Nugget Gift Shop were places she'd passed before finding somewhere to have breakfast.

The old man next to her tapped her on the shoulder. "Would you pass that cream over here?" He pointed to the stainless pitcher just out of his reach.

"Sure." She moved the pitcher in front of him.

"Thanks." He winked at Jessie. "I like a little coffee with my cream." He poured a generous amount of liquid in his coffee mug and stirred it carefully with his spoon.

"I can see that."

"Are you the little gal who's supposed to be the singer?"

Jess pushed her empty plate away and picked up her coffee. "Well, I could be, I guess. Who am I supposed to be?"

"Well, I'm not sure," he drawled, his blue eyes twinkling. "I'm a Hank Williams fan myself."

Jess held out her hand. "I'm Jessie Carter. And I like Hank Williams, too."

"Amos Barstow."

The waitress picked up Jessie's plate. "Watch out for him," she winked. "He's an old flirt."

"Not so old," Amos objected, dropping Jessie's hand. "This lady is that singer Grace told us about."

"No kidding! You're really Jessie Carter?"

"Yes," Jess agreed. "Who's Grace?"

"Grace Perkins. She works at the hotel."

"Oh." Jess spoke without thinking. "Dan must have told her who I was."

Amos winked at her. "So you know Dan, do you?"

The waitress claimed Jessie's attention. "Do you know Reba McIntyre?"

"I've met her a couple of times, but—"

"Don't you think she's getting too skinny?" The waitress shook her head. "Nothing but skin and bones. And you're not much bigger yourself."

"I ate breakfast," Jessie said, conscious of how much weight she'd lost in the past year. She couldn't remember when food had tasted good, and the energy she put into her performances melted the pounds away.

"And you should do it more often, too," the woman pointed out.

"Don't let her boss you," Amos growled. "Maizie is full of opinions, most of them not worth listening to."

Jessie laughed, and took another sip of coffee. What a luxury it was to linger over breakfast and know the whole day was hers to spend as she wished. She didn't have to be anywhere, didn't have to perform tonight. Didn't have to do anything she didn't want to do.

"So, Miss Jessie," Amos began, "what do you think of our little town?"

"I like it very much."

"We've been around since 1859, you know, when they first found gold. You can still see some of the mines in the hills behind town, not too far away. Course we didn't get gambling 'til four years ago. Sure made a difference around here."

"We used to be a ghost town. Now we're a tourist town," Maizie explained. "You ever been to Colorado before?"

"Just once, a few years ago."

"Are you singing around here somewhere?" the man to the left of her asked. He was slightly younger than Amos, with more hair and darker eyes.

"No. I'm on vacation."

"That's too bad. We'd sure enjoy hearing you sing. My daughter likes your songs."

"I'm glad she does, but I'm taking a break from performing for a while."

The man pushed a clean napkin toward her, along with a pen. "Can I have your autograph?"

"Sure." Jessie scrawled her name and the date on the piece of paper and gave it back to him. She had never stopped being surprised at being asked for her autograph. She always wanted to ask "Are you talking to me?"

Amos leaned closer, his eyes full of mischief. "How do you know Dan?"

"I met him four years ago, when he was a deputy south of here."

"Before he inherited the hotel, then," Amos stated.

"Yes, that's right."

"That was a sad day, when Susie and Wade were killed. Never did trust those little planes."

"Susie and Wade?"

"His brother and sister-in-law." Amos frowned. "I thought you knew Dan."

"We haven't exactly kept in touch." Jess took another sip of her coffee. "Dan took over the hotel when they died?"

"Yes, and took care of their little girl, too."

Jessie swallowed hard and turned toward the old man. "Dan isn't married?"

Maizie heard her question and laughed. "Dan? Married?"

Amos chuckled, too. "No. I heard he'd been married once, but he never talks about it. He's quite the ladies' man, but no one around here's been able to pin him down."

Jessie picked up her coffee cup and settled in for a long conversation.

"HAS MS. CARTER checked out yet?"

"Just a minute, Dan. I'll see." Grace flipped through several receipts. "If she left before ten, Jeff would have handled it."

Dan looked at his watch. Checkout time was noon. Jessie had seven minutes to get her ass down to the lobby or pay for another day.

"No," Grace said after a long minute. "Was she planning to leave this morning?"

"I thought so. Maybe you should call her and see if she needs help with her bags."

"I will not. She could still be sleeping. You look terrible. Are you feeling okay?"

"Never better, Grace." In fact, he'd had a tough morning. He hadn't slept well at all, which irritated him. He wasn't usually so restless in his sleep. Another reason to want Jessie Carter gone.

Grace didn't look as if she believed him. She was like a mother to him, but she didn't push. "If you say so," she mumbled. "But if I were you, I'd get to bed early tonight."

"I'll do that, Grace," he promised, eyeing the staircase.

"Reservations for next weekend have picked up."

"What?" No one came down the stairs.

Grace repeated the information about the reservations. "Are you sure you're feeling all right?"

Maybe he should ring her room. Or better yet, go up there and find out for himself when she was going to leave. Maybe he could carry her bags for her. He'd done it before.

"I *said*, are you feeling all right?"

"What?" Dan turned back to the desk and to the woman who frowned at him. "Did you ask me something?"

Grace shook her head. "Maybe you should go get some fresh air."

"Why?" He glanced toward the staircase again. She had three minutes left. Where the hell was she? And why would she stay another day in a small town like this? He heard Grace say something, but he didn't stop to listen. Instead, he went up the staircase, taking the stairs two at a time until he reached the third floor. It took about three seconds to reach the door to Jessie's room, and three minutes to decide whether or not to knock. Then Dan remembered staring at the ceiling until four o'clock and felt no guilt about waking Jessie.

He waited for an answer to his knock, but there was silence on the other side of the door. He knocked again, louder this time. The hall was empty; although the second floor was full, only three out of ten rooms on this floor were occupied.

"Jess," he called.

"Are you looking for me, lawman?" said a familiar voice behind him. Dan turned to see Jess step toward him in the corridor. She wore tight jeans tucked into an expensive-looking pair of black cowboy boots, and a black sweatshirt. As she came closer, he could see the shirt was decorated with rhinestone musical notes. Her hair was loose this morning, a yellow mass brushing her shoulders.

She was still pale.

"Yes. I thought you were checking out."

She pulled a key from her pocket and moved to the door. "I'd planned to, but..." She unlocked the door and it swung open.

"But?" Dan followed her into the room and shut the door behind him.

She shot him an amused look. "I have this sense of déjà vu."

He didn't smile. "Do you need help with your bags?"

"A suitcase and an old guitar? I don't think so. Besides," she drawled, perching on the bed, "I've decided to stay for awhile longer."

"How long is 'awhile'?"

"I don't know." She tilted her head. "Why does my staying bother you?"

"It doesn't."

"Yes, it does. You're not being honest with me."

"Is honesty a requirement for this conversation?"

"I think so."

"Why did you come back to Colorado, Jessie?"

"You want an *honest* answer?"

"Yeah." He braced himself for the worst. She'd returned for the child, now that she was rich and famous and could afford to take care of a baby, despite everything she'd said last night about being happy the child had found a home.

"Well, you're not going to get one, at least not now." She smoothed her palm along the chenille bedspread and didn't meet his gaze.

In one step he was in front of her, and had lifted her chin with his hand so she had to look up at him. There was no fear in her expression, only a deep pain that shocked him. She covered it quickly, trying to smile.

"Tell me, Jessie. I won't leave until you do." He dropped his hand from her face before he could be tempted to bend down and kiss her. He didn't want to kiss her; he refused to feel anything for her.

"I wondered what happened to you," she whispered. "So I went to the diner, but it was closed up. Your cabin was, too."

"Gus was too ill to handle it any more. He died last year."

"I'm sorry. He was kind to me."

"Why aren't you working? Don't you have concerts and TV appearances and things like that to do?"

"Concerts, yes. Television, sometimes. I told you last night, I'm on vacation."

"I didn't believe you." She hadn't asked about the baby again. Maybe he was wrong; maybe she didn't have any connection to the child at all. "What are you doing here?"

"I wanted to know what had happened to you, and to Jane," Jess explained.

Dan ignored the reference to the child. "Did you think I would be in that cabin, waiting for you?" He couldn't hide the bitterness in his voice.

"No." Her voice faltered. "I didn't stop to think. I guess I wondered if what we had that night was real or if I'd imagined it."

Dan stepped back. "So we're still being honest?"

She gazed up at him, trying to understand.

"There is nothing for you here," he said, his voice rough as he turned to look at her once again. "Is that honest enough for you?"

He slammed the door behind him.

JESS SKIPPED LUNCH and took a nap as thick clouds covered the afternoon sun. Then she strolled along Main Street. She lost three dollars at the Gold Digger and won five at Molly Malone's. She decided she liked slot machines. She bought a souvenir T-shirt and postcards, and stood outside the Gold City Opera House and wondered why the ornate brick building looked unused.

There were worse places to spend the winter, she decided, walking back to the hotel. The mountain air made her sleepy, something she appreciated. The people were friendly. All except Dan, that is. And she didn't understand why he'd care one way or another. He had his hotel and his little girl and his life in this town.

Jess went inside the hotel and asked Grace for her key.

Grace hurried to get it for her. "Did you find everything you were looking for?"

"I sure did." Jess held up her package. "Bought some souvenirs, too."

"I'm glad you're having a good time." She lowered her voice, leaning forward. "You know, Kevin Costner stayed here once."

"Really?" Jessie didn't have time to go to the movies, but she certainly knew who Kevin Costner was. "What was he doing in Colorado?"

"I think he was researching a movie." Grace sighed. "He was very quiet, so we left him alone. He was only here overnight."

Jess wondered if he'd found inspiration. She could certainly use some.

"Still here, Ms. Carter?" a familiar voice drawled behind her. Jess turned to see Dan coming toward her.

"Yes," she said, her tone polite. Grace would be hanging on to every word. "I'm enjoying your town."

"You're a gambler, then."

"I've been known to take a few chances, yes." They both knew she wasn't talking about slot machines.

"And how long will you be staying?"

Jess refused to let him intimidate her into leaving before she was damn ready. "I haven't decided, Sheriff."

"You must be used to more exciting places than Gold City. You're not bored?"

"Dan!" Grace scolded. "How can you say that?"

Dan glanced toward the desk. "I'm going to pick up Anna."

"Tell Beth I'll drop by after work."

"Excuse me," Jess said, moving out of the way. She

couldn't bear to stand there a moment longer and have
Dan treat her like a stranger. She was still attracted to
him. She kept wishing she could fall into his arms and
have him hold her while she told him about the last
four years. She wanted to tell him how tired she was,
how the songs didn't dance in her head anymore, why
she was so afraid she'd never write another one. She'd
foolishly thought she could find her lawman in Colorado and he would comfort her and tell her everything
would be all right.

What a stupid idea. She'd laugh if it didn't hurt so
much.

Jessie hesitated before the staircase. The lounge on
her left looked cozy and inviting. She'd have a glass of
wine and contemplate her future.

"DON'T TELL." Anna scooped a scrawny calico kitten
into her arms and held it against her chest. "Please?"

Jessie looked behind her. The corridor was empty.
"Don't tell *who?*"

The little girl hugged the kitten tighter. "Don't tell
*anyone*. And don't tell Daddy."

Jess knelt down so that she was on eye level with the
child and her pet. She reached out and stroked the kitten's head. "Don't tell anyone about the kitten? Why
not?"

Anna nodded. "I can't have a kitty."

"You can't? Why not?"

"Daddy said."

"Oh." The kitten meowed, a pitiful cry that seemed
loud in the empty corridor. "Then why do you have
it?"

"I found it," Anna whispered. "He was crying outside."

"You don't think he belongs to anyone?" Even as she asked the question, she knew how ridiculous it was. This little animal looked anything but well fed and cared for.

"Uh-uh."

"Did you just find him?"

The child nodded. "By my sandbox."

"Maybe we'd better find something for him to eat. Where's your Daddy?"

"Downstairs."

"Are you supposed to be in your room?"

Anna nodded.

"Okay." She peeled the kitten from Anna's shirt. "Let me put this little guy in my room for now. He's going to need something to eat." And someplace to go to the bathroom. Jessie held the kitten away from her shirt as she stood up and picked up her purse and her package. "You should be in your room, if that's where your father told you to be."

The little girl gazed up at her with wide gray eyes. "Can I keep him?"

"I don't know. Let's get him something to eat and then we'll figure something out."

"Promise you won't tell Daddy?"

Jessie nodded. "Promise. Show me where your room is so I can find you when I get back."

The little girl led her around the corner to a separate wing of the hotel. She pointed to a large door marked Private. "That's my house." Her expression grew serious. "My name is Anna MacAdams."

"I'll knock when I get back, Anna. I'm Jessie, and I'm in room 315."

"'Kay." The child looked longingly at the kitten before she moved toward her door. Jessie waited for the child to be safely inside before she returned to her room with the crying kitten. She put the kitten on the floor and prayed the thing wouldn't mess on the carpet.

It looked at her and mewed piteously. Jess picked it up and put it in the bathroom, then put a towel on the floor. "Why don't you take a nice nap?"

The kitten cried once again, then sat down on its haunches. "Good kitty," Jess told it, and shut the door. How had she gotten herself into this? One glass of wine and she was rescuing kittens. And she'd never liked cats. She slung her purse over her shoulder once again and tried to remember if she'd seen a grocery store nearby.

Thirty minutes later Jess had accomplished her mission. Dan and Grace were hunched over the computer at the front desk, so Jess assumed Anna was still in her room where she was supposed to be. Once back in 315, Jess opened the bathroom door. The little kitten lay curled in the bath towel as if she'd lived there forever. There was no evidence of any mess, thank goodness. "Come on," Jess told it, scooping it into her arms. "Time to go visit your new owner."

She hurried down the hall and around the corner. She tapped on the door. "It's me. Jessie," she whispered. The child opened the door and burst into a wide smile when she saw the kitten. She held out her arms and Jess handed her the little animal.

"I bought it some food, but I don't know how you're going to keep it without telling your father," Jessie warned, stepping inside the large room. The carpet was the same gold color as the one in Jessie's room, but the curtains that covered the tall windows were lace. Two ivory love seats faced each other, a cherry butler's table between them, and bookcases filled the wall on either side of the fireplace. A cherry dining-room table and chairs filled the other side of the room. She couldn't picture Dan living in this room. "Where's the kitchen? We should put some of this food in a dish."

"Okay." Anna led her through a door to the right into a small kitchen. She pointed to the white cupboard next to the sink. "Up there."

Jessie opened the simple cabinet and found a saucer and a cereal bowl. She opened two drawers before she found a can opener. She felt a little uncomfortable, as if she was trespassing in Dan's life.

"He looks like the Lion King," Anna said.

Jessie poured a little cream into the bowl. "Where are you going to keep it?"

"In your room?"

"Nope. The maid would find it in the morning when she cleans."

"Mary won't tell," Anna assured her. She wrinkled her nose. "What food is that?"

"I don't know. Some kind of cat food. I thought it might like something soft." Jess set both dishes on the floor. "Put him down and see what he does."

The little kitten sniffed the dishes, lapped the cream until the bowl was empty, then took a tentative taste of the food before eagerly devouring the rest. Anna sat beside him on the floor and watched his every move. "He likes it!"

Jess figured a starving cat would appreciate anything at all, but she didn't say so. "He sure does."

When the kitten finished, he licked his paws clean and purred.

"He's so cute," Anna moaned.

Jessie sat beside her on the floor and leaned against

the refrigerator. "Why won't your father let you have a cat?"

Anna shrugged. "I dunno."

"Did you ask him?"

Anna nodded. "He said no."

Well, that was clear enough. Jessie couldn't think of anything else she could do. After all, she wasn't one of Dan MacAdams's favorite people. She shouldn't be sitting in his kitchen, helping his daughter deceive him. She should be in her room looking at travel brochures. "You have to tell him, Anna. Maybe he'll change his mind."

"I dunno," the child sighed. "I don't think he likes kitties."

Jess didn't like kitties too much herself, but the little girl's enthusiasm was hard to resist. "Maybe the kitty could stay outside until you talk to your father."

"Uh-uh. He might run away. I'll put him in my room." She picked him up and kissed his head. "Come, little Simba."

"I'll clean up," Jess offered, climbing to her feet. She tossed the empty can into the garbage where it wouldn't be seen, then tucked the carton of cream into the back of the refrigerator behind a jar of pickles. She washed the two dishes and wiped them dry with a paper towel before replacing them in the cupboard. Then she followed Anna's voice to her bedroom and paused in the doorway. "Anna?"

The child sat in the middle of a small bed, the kitten cradled in her lap. She was singing it a song and petting its head.

"Anna?" Jess repeated.

The little girl looked up and smiled. "He's sleeping!"

"It's almost dinnertime," Jessie pointed out. "I have to go now."

"'Bye." Anna waved. "Thank you for the food."

"You're welcome, Anna."

Jess backed out of the bedroom and hurried around the living room corner to face the stunned expression of Dan MacAdams. She felt her heart jump. He looked as if he'd seen a ghost, a ghost he didn't particularly like.

"What the hell are you doing here?" he barked.

She looked up into those familiar dark eyes and refused to be intimidated. "I was invited," she snapped. She started to move past him toward the door. "Now, if you'll excuse me..."

He grabbed her elbow. "No way. You can't have her, Jessie. It's too late."

"What are you talking about?"

His face was close to hers. "You can't waltz back in here and think you're going to take her away from me. I won't let it happen, do you understand?"

Jessie shook his hand from her arm. "I don't know what you're talking about, lawman. But maybe the altitude has affected your brain."

"Look," he pointed to a wall of framed photographs near the front door. "Don't play dumb."

Jess walked over to examine the photographs. A smiling couple posed with a toddler in several of them. And then she saw it. The dark-haired couple with the baby. A baby whose round face and blue eyes looked remarkably familiar. Jess turned back to Dan. "Jane?"

"You didn't know?"

"Of course not." She peered closer. "This must have been taken shortly after I found her."

"It was. Her foster parents were my brother and sister-in-law. They later adopted her."

"And then they died," Jessie added. At Dan's surprised expression, she explained. "Someone at the coffee shop told me the story. But I didn't realize that Anna was the child I'd left with you."

"I was her godfather. Their will left everything to me, including Anna."

Jess peered at the pictures again. "Amazing," she murmured. "I wondered so many times what had happened to her." She turned back to Dan. "You thought I'd come back for her. Why?"

"We never found the hitchhiker. In fact, there was never any evidence a hitchhiker existed."

"But the waitress in Granby—"

"Said you looked enough alike to be sisters, and she couldn't tell whose baby it was, though she remembered your searching for the girl after she left."

"She was a hitchhiker," Jess insisted. "And she left the baby with me."

"You don't want her back?"

"She's not mine," Jessie insisted. "She never was."

The lines around his mouth eased, but his gaze was sharp. "Then why are you in my living room?"

Jessie couldn't help smiling. "Looks like your daughter is more like her father than you know. She's found a stray she's determined to keep."

"What's that supposed to mean?"

"Daddy!" Anna burst out of the bedroom, the kitten snuggled in her arms. "Look what I found!"

# 6

"ARE YOU SURE you wouldn't like a glass of wine?" Inviting her to dinner seemed the least he could do for the woman who said she wasn't going to try to take his daughter away. Dan wanted to believe her, wanted to believe that she was here to rest, as she'd insisted. But he had the gut feeling there was something more to it, something she wasn't saying. Not that he expected her to tell him everything about her life.

They'd been lovers for one night only, four long years ago.

He had to keep remembering that it hadn't meant anything. He had to keep reminding himself to put it out of his mind.

"I'm sure." She gave him that devastating smile of hers, the one he recognized from the cover of her latest CD. She'd insisted on changing out of her jeans before joining them in the dining room. Now she wore tight black knit pants, a long gold sweater that hung to her thighs, and black cowboy boots with a yellow flower-petal pattern. Gold hoops swung from her ears. She'd looked like someone special when she'd strode across the dining room to their table and people had stared.

"Are you still thinking, Daddy?" Anna asked.

"What?" He reluctantly tore his gaze away from Jessie and turned to his daughter.

"The kitty," she prompted.

"I'm still thinking," he stated. "I don't know about keeping a kitten cooped up in our apartment all day. It doesn't seem fair to the kitten."

"Kitties like beds," Anna insisted.

"Finish your carrots."

Anna obediently stabbed a vegetable and lifted it to her mouth. "Can he sleep with me tonight?"

Jess chuckled. "She doesn't give up, does she?"

"No." He sighed. "The dirt in the shoe box had better work."

"You can buy a litter box tomorrow," Jessie assured him. "Every little girl needs a kitten."

"Did you have one?"

"Well, no," she admitted. "I had a dog."

God help him, he was still attracted to her. It was all he could do to cut his steak and lift the meat to his mouth. He forced himself to chew and swallow as if he was completely unaffected by having dinner with her.

He kept remembering her body beneath his, how he fit snugly inside of her, the way she'd kissed him. He cleared his throat. "I did, too."

"But kittens are nice, too," she assured Anna. "They're much happier to be inside the house, and you don't have to take them for walks."

They looked alike, Dan noted once again. Yellow hair, gray eyes, ravishing smiles. Anna's face was much rounder, while Jessie's was oval, the cheekbones obvious. The dark shadows still marred the skin under her eyes, and her skin was still pale. Being a star didn't look as if it agreed with her. She continued to watch Anna with great delight, as if she couldn't believe her good fortune in finding the child once again. But there was nothing maternal in the expression, no motherly gestures or cautious possessiveness.

The caution was all on his part, and he felt foolish for worrying so much. He needed to lighten up, just as Grace delighted in advising him. He would try for normal, everyday conversation, he decided. "What do you think of Gold City?"

"I like it," she replied. "The people are so friendly."

"It can get a little noisy at night."

"I'm used to noise."

"Yes, I guess you are. Are you on the road a lot?"

"Most of the year. We've been traveling on the bus for more days than I want to admit. The past couple of years have been a blur."

"But you got what you wanted."

"Yes." She didn't look at him, but wiped her lips with her napkin.

"Then why aren't you happy?"

"Who says I'm not happy?"

He shrugged. "Just a feeling I have. As if you're not telling the whole truth."

Anna tugged on her father's arm. "Ice cream?"

"In a minute, when we've all finished our dinners." He turned back to Jessie, hoping she wouldn't get up and leave. She looked as if she'd like to. "Is there anything I can help you with?"

She smiled. "Always the rescuer, aren't you?" Dan couldn't argue with her, so he didn't try. "You can't help me with this one, lawman."

"I could try." He had the craziest urge to reach across the table and take her hand, so he gripped his fork.

"I'll let you know," she said. "Thank you for dinner. I appreciate the company."

"Was the food all right?"

"Delicious." She pushed her plate away slightly, and

the waitress hurried over to remove it. "I swear, food tastes better in Colorado. I'm going to have to buy new clothes when I go back on tour."

"And when is that?"

"I'm not sure." She looked at Anna. "Do you have ice cream every night?"

The child shook her head. "Sometimes I have a cookie."

"You're a lucky girl," Jess told her.

Anna nodded. "Do kitties like ice cream?"

"I would think so."

Dan groaned. "Don't tell me I have to bring ice cream upstairs to a stray cat."

"Would you care for dessert, Mr. MacAdams?" the waitress asked.

"What would you like, Jess?"

"Just a cup of decaf coffee, thank you."

"For me, too," he told Sarah. "And a small dish of vanilla ice cream for Anna, and one to take upstairs."

Sarah quickly brought the coffee and ice cream.

Dan poured too much sugar in his coffee before he noticed he wasn't paying attention.

Jess took a sip of her coffee. "Do you eat here every night?"

"Almost. It's easier for both of us this way."

"I can imagine."

"Anna goes to preschool every morning, then Grace's daughter picks her up and takes her home with her for the afternoon. It works out well for all of us, although Beth is expecting her first child in February. I don't know if that will change things or not."

"She wants a girl," Anna announced. "Just like me."

"I'm sure she does," Jessie said, smiling at her.

"Who wouldn't?" Then, as if she realized what she'd said, she looked at Dan. "I shouldn't have—"

"That's okay. I ask myself that same question every so often."

They finished their coffee in silence, collected a small container of ice cream and headed upstairs. Anna insisted Jessie look at the kitten again, and the little girl sat on the floor and watched the cat take tentative licks from the container.

"Stay here, honey," Dan told her. "I'm going to take Jessie back to her room."

Jess protested. "You don't have—"

"I insist," he said, guiding her toward the door. The sweater was soft against the palm of his hand as he touched her back.

Jess hesitated. "'Bye, Anna. Maybe I'll see you tomorrow."

"'Bye, Jessie!"

Dan didn't want to like her. He didn't want to think about her at all. She was an acquaintance; she was a guest in his hotel. Inviting her to dinner had been insane. Almost as insane as keeping a stray kitten.

Dan walked Jess down the corridor and around the corner to her room. They stopped in front of the door while Jessie fumbled in her purse for the key.

"You don't believe me, do you?"

"Believe what?" Of course he knew what she meant.

"That I'm not Anna's mother." She unlocked the door and Dan followed her inside without waiting for an invitation.

"I'd like to believe it." He looked right into those clear gray eyes of hers, wondering if he would be able to tell if she lied. If she was here to claim her daughter, she could have her own reasons for not admitting it.

"You believed me that night of the storm."

"I hadn't checked out your story yet. Later I realized it was a pretty strange set of circumstances. I wondered if you'd left her so you could go to Nashville without another mouth to feed."

"I would never have done anything like that," Jess insisted. "I did everything I could to keep that baby safe, including spending the night at your cabin."

He didn't want to talk about that night. "I know."

"Is there anything I can do to convince you?"

"You can leave." He saw the flash of disappointment in her eyes and felt a pang of guilt.

"All right," she agreed. "If that's what it takes. Funny, I don't remember you as particularly cruel," she said. "Except the morning I left. You had my bags by the door and the snow shovelled before I finished taking a shower. You had been so...kind the night before. And then you couldn't wait to get rid of me." Her voice grew husky. "Just like now."

"I don't like goodbyes."

"No one does, lawman." She waved one delicate hand toward the door. "Good night."

He didn't move. Couldn't move. "Jessie..."

She put her hands on her hips. "What do you want from me, Dan? I told you, I'm on vacation. I don't want anything from—"

He cut off her words by pulling her to him and bringing his lips to hers. Dan felt her surprise, and the flare of passion that burst between them. He lifted his mouth from hers before he did anything he'd regret.

"Why?" she whispered.

"I should have done that the morning you left, four years ago."

"You did."

"Then I should have made love to you again."

She tucked a stray strand of hair behind her ear. "Yes. You should have."

"Would you have stayed?"

"I don't know."

Dan cupped her face with gentle hands. "Go back to Nashville, Jess. Or wherever it is you call home," he murmured. Her skin was like porcelain, fine and clear. "We were wrong for each other four years ago and we still are."

He placed a quick kiss on her lips before dropping his hands from her face and turning to the door. He left swiftly, before he could change his mind.

Jess shut the door behind him and locked it with shaking fingers. He wanted her to leave; she wanted to stay. He thought she'd come for Anna; she'd come for something—someone—else.

He thought they were wrong for each other; she'd thought four years ago that he was the best thing that had ever happened to her. She'd hoped they could be friends; he'd kissed her like a frustrated lover.

His life was here. Hers wasn't, she reminded herself. And never could be.

Suddenly she felt like crying. Her old guitar waited for her in the corner of the room, but Jessie didn't pick it up. The music was gone and she didn't know what to do, but leaving Gold City wasn't the answer. Running away wouldn't help. And, God help her, she was still attracted to Dan MacAdams, but she was four years older, four years wiser. Their night together had been something special, something she'd never repeated.

It was time she got over it.

JESSIE HANDED Amos the pitcher of cream and explained exactly what she needed. "Nothing big," she said. "I don't need a lot of room."

"Hmm." The old man stroked his chin. "There are a couple of places that might work. Let's see, the Simms house just west of the grocery store might still be empty."

Maizie shook her head. "Not anymore. They rented it a couple of weeks ago, to those people from Colorado Springs."

"Too bad."

"Can you think of anything else?"

"Have you talked to Grace at the hotel?"

"No. Should I?"

"I think there's a house near her daughter's that might be for rent." He swivelled on his stool as Dan walked into the coffee shop. "Dan!"

Jess winced. He was the last person she wanted to see this morning. In fact, she'd hurried out of the hotel early so she wouldn't run into him.

"Amos." He stopped near them and shot Jessie a curious look. "Good morning, Jessie."

"Good morning."

"Sit down, son," Amos said, pointing to the empty stool beside him. "This young lady and I were just talking about finding her a house to rent."

Dan paused, then slid onto the stool. "For how long?"

The question was addressed to Amos, but Jessie answered it. "I'm not sure. Maybe until the first of the year."

"I don't think anyone will want to rent for that short a time."

"I'd lease it for longer if I had to."

Amos chuckled. "Looks like she's anxious to leave the Gold Bar, Dan. You're about to lose a customer."

"I don't mind," he stated. "Maizie, could I have a cup of coffee and a cinnamon roll?"

"Comin' up!"

"You walk down South Street every day, don't you?"

Dan nodded, and fixed his coffee.

"Isn't something for rent down there?" Amos prodded.

Dan took a cautious sip from the mug. "Seems that the simplest thing to do would be go to the real estate office, over by Molly Malone's."

Amos frowned at him. "And ruin my conversation with a gen-u-ine country-western singer?"

Jessie pulled some money from her wallet and laid it on the counter. She slid off the stool and slung her purse over her shoulder. "That's okay, Amos. You've given me some ideas." She looked over at Dan. "Thanks. I'll head over to the real estate office now."

"They're not open until ten."

"I'll take a walk. Maybe I'll see something for rent."

Dan stood up. "Maizie, save this for me. I'll be back in a minute."

Amos touched her arm. "Don't forget, you promised to help with the Harvest Dinner."

"I won't forget. I'm a pretty good dishwasher," she assured him. Dan followed her out of the coffee shop, his hand on her back as he guided her down the boardwalk to the corner. Then he stopped and stood in front of her. "About last night, Jessie..."

She was over him, she reminded herself. Completely over him. "What about it?"

"I need to apologize. I never meant to hurt you."

"It doesn't matter," Jessie lied.

"I shouldn't have told you to leave." He took a deep breath. "What you do or where you go is none of my business."

"I'll be checking out of the hotel as soon as I find a place to live."

He frowned. "Why would you want to live in Gold City? What the hell are you thinking about?"

Obviously he'd decided it was his business after all. "This has nothing to do with you or Anna. I'm thinking about getting some rest, some fresh air and some decent, home-cooked food. About sleeping at night in the same bed and wearing old clothes and not having to ride a bus to the next gig. Does that explain it?"

"It might." He paused, his expression softening. "You look like hell."

"I know." She sighed. "I've been riding a roller coaster for the past few years."

"The price of fame," he noted.

"Yeah." She stuck her hand out. "Truce? I'll stay out of your way, you stay out of mine."

Dan took her hand and she was amazed at how gentle his fingers were. "You mean, this town is big enough for both of us?"

She returned the smile. "That's a real lawman kind of thing to say."

"Maybe you should write a song about it," he teased.

Jessie laughed. It felt good to stand in the cool morning sunshine and hold hands with the good-looking man she'd thought of so often. "Maybe I should," she agreed. "You'll be the first to know."

"Well," he said, releasing his grip, "let me know how you make out with a house."

"Your coffee's getting cold," she reminded him.

"Take care of yourself, Jessie."

"Sure." She watched as he turned around and walked back inside the coffee shop. That was that, she told herself. From now on she would forget him and get on with her life. She'd returned to Colorado for some peace and quiet, not to find a lover.

"ARE YOU SURE you want to be on the cleanup committee?"

Jessie sat at her new neighbor's kitchen table and sipped her tea. "Sure. It'll be a nice change to be 'backstage' for once."

Beth chewed the end of her pencil and studied the pad in front of her. She didn't look at all like her mother, Jess thought. Dark curly hair to her chin and a heart-shaped face with big brown eyes made her look like a pregnant elf. She was tiny, with a belly that looked as if she had shoved a small basketball under her oversize knit shirt. "I don't know," she muttered. "Seems like you should be master of ceremonies or something important."

"I'll donate some CDs to the raffle," Jessie offered, hoping that would appease her new neighbor. It had taken less than a week to find a house, arrange to lease it, and move her few belongings from room 315 to the two-bedroom cottage on the ridge behind Main Street. Grace's elderly mother had died six months ago, and the family couldn't decide what to do with the house. No one in the family wanted to live in it, and no one in the family wanted to sell it, either, Grace had explained. So they'd put the personal possessions in the attic, polished the furniture and scrubbed the place until it shone. Jess had been in the house for only a week, and felt as if she'd lived there all her life.

"They'll be selling dances afterwards, you know." Beth eyed Jessie speculatively. "I'll bet your dance card would raise a lot of money."

"I draw the line."

"Too bad. The Opera House could use the donations."

"Don't try to make me feel guilty, Beth." Jess picked up another cookie. "Bribing me with sugar cookies won't do it either."

Beth patted her belly and yawned. "I feel like baking all the time. Mom says it's a nesting instinct. Ten weeks to go, thank goodness."

Jessie looked at her watch. "Do you want me to get Anna for you? It's almost time."

Beth gave her a grateful look. "That would really help. I am so tired today. I don't know why. And I don't think the meatballs I ate last night agreed with me."

"Should you see a doctor?"

Beth chuckled. "No. I might lie down for a few minutes, though." She stood up slowly and winced.

"Beth?"

Beth waved Jess away. "I'm okay. Just a little tired."

"Go lie down. Anna and I will be back in a few minutes, and if you're asleep I'll feed her lunch at my house."

"You don't mind?"

"Of course not."

It didn't take long to walk to the preschool, collect Anna and the day's artwork, and stroll back up the hill toward home. Anna held Jessie's hand and chattered about her friends and the kitten. Jessie couldn't believe she was the baby from the storm; and yet, the ready smile and sparkling eyes were the same. The child was still a little charmer.

"Where's Beth?"

"She's having a rest," Jess explained as they approached the house. "Be very quiet, in case she's asleep. We don't want to wake her up."

They tiptoed into the house and saw Beth asleep on the couch. Anna started to giggle, but clapped her hand over her mouth in time. Jessie took her hand and led her out of the house and across the yard.

"I like your house," Anna said, a few minutes later. She had consented to eat her sandwich in the kitchen, at the tiny table tucked underneath a window that overlooked the valley.

"Thank you." Jess put a glass of milk beside the child's plate.

"My kitty would like it. Can he come visit?"

"Sure. I'd like the company." Jess hadn't expected to feel lonely, but the nights were too long and too quiet. She'd been grateful for Beth's friendship and breakfasts with Amos at the coffee shop. Sometimes Dan was there at the same time and he said hello.

And she said hello back.

That was the extent of her social life.

"Wanna color?" Anna asked.

"I don't have any crayons."

"I do. In my backpack." She turned to the hot pink bag hanging over the back of the chair. "Do you play Go Fish?"

"You can teach me. Eat your lunch first." Jess looked at her watch. She should let Dan know where Anna was, so he wouldn't call Beth and wake her up if he wanted to talk to his daughter.

Anna knew the phone number of the hotel, so Jessie called and reached Grace, who was concerned about her daughter and promised to give Dan the message that Anna was with Jessie.

The phone rang three minutes later, just as Anna finished her milk.

"Hello?"

"Jess? It's Dan." Worry tinged his voice. "I'll be over to get Anna as soon as I can."

"You don't have to," Jessie assured him. "We're fine. She's going to teach me to play Go Fish."

"That's not at all necessary."

"Yes, it is." Jessie kept her voice light, hoping he wouldn't reject her once again. "I don't have a clue how it goes."

Silence. Then, "Are you sure?"

"Positive. If it's okay with you, we might get the kitten and bring it back here to play in the yard."

"I'd love to get rid of that cat," he muttered. "The damn thing is wrecking the curtains and the furniture. Just a minute."

She heard a muffled conversation, then Dan came back to the phone. "Grace wants to check on Beth, so I need to stay here at the desk. I have two busloads of senior citizens here for the next two days, so one of us has to stay. Are you sure you don't mind baby-sitting?"

"Not at all. Beth seemed awfully tired. Do you think everything's okay?"

"She'll be fine," he assured her. "And, Jess? Thanks again."

"It's really nothing," Jessie said, meaning the words. Having Anna for a few hours filled an otherwise lonely afternoon. She loved having time to read, the freedom to take long walks and the luxury of sleeping in the same place each night, but she longed for more contact with people. Drinking coffee beside Amos was often the highlight of her day. "We'll have fun."

After lunch Jessie and Anna walked to the hotel and hurried up the back staircase to get the kitten. They peeked into the lobby and saw a line at the reception desk but no sign of Grace. Dan looked too busy to interrupt, though he smiled and waved at them, so Jessie tugged Anna out the door toward home. The kitten seemed content to be carried in the girl's arms, but at Jessie's house Anna let him run free in the fenced backyard.

"Simba likes your house," the child said.

"Yes," Jessie agreed, and absentmindedly watched the kitten swat a bug from a stalk of grass. Dan had smiled at her. He had waved and smiled as she'd taken his daughter and led her from the hotel. Her heart had lifted three inches. Maybe friendship was possible after all.

"Jessie?" Grace stood on Beth's back porch and waved.

"Stay here with Simba," Jessie told Anna. "I'll be right back." She went to the fence and Grace hurried across the grass. "Is everything okay?"

Grace didn't smile. "I don't know. I'm taking Beth to the doctor now. She's having labor pains."

"What does that mean?"

"She's only six-and-a-half months along, which is too soon for the baby to be born. Maybe the doctor will put her in the hospital. I don't know." Grace looked as if she was going to cry.

Jessie put her hand on Grace's shoulder. "Is there anything I can do?"

"No," Grace sniffed. "I've called Ken. He's going to meet us at the doctor's office." She looked over Jessie's shoulder to where Anna sat on the grass. "Thanks for taking care of Anna. I know Dan appreciates it."

"I don't mind at all. Tell Beth I hope she feels better."

"I will," Grace said, moving away from the fence toward the house. Jessie turned back to Anna.

"Are you cold?"

"I have a coat on."

Jess shivered. She could feel the chill of winter on the back of her neck. "I'm going inside," she told Anna. "What about you?"

"We're playing," Anna told her, not bothering to turn around. "It's nice here."

It was nice, Jessie had to agree. The yard was small, yet held a clothesline and toolshed. Grace's mother had obviously liked to garden at one time, because empty flowerbeds were tucked beneath the picket fence and bushes provided privacy at the far end of the yard. "Come in when you get cold," Jessie told her. "I'll be watching you out the window."

She went up the steps to the back door and hurried inside the warm kitchen. This was the way most people lived, snug in a house with children and cups of tea and their own bed each night. It made a nice change from life on the road. Of course, it wasn't as exciting as singing for hundreds or thousands of enthusiastic fans, but she was getting the rest she needed. And someday, she assured herself, the music would come back and she would be able to return to her real life.

the kitten on her lap. "I wish there were more I could do," she said.

Jessie went to one of the stove, stirred something in a pot. When she turned to him again she seemed to relax. "It'll be finished in a few minutes."

Dan leaned forward, resting his chin on the

---

# 7

DAN ARRIVED at Jessie's house promptly at five o'clock, unwilling to impose on her any longer than he had to. The tourists had all been checked into their rooms and, as he'd left the hotel, he'd noticed they'd begun to file into the dining room. Jeff could handle things at the hotel now, though. As sheriff, he was also off duty unless something came up the deputies couldn't handle.

He hurried up the steps and knocked on the front door. Anna would be waiting for him. She was probably upset over the change in her routine.

"Come on in," Jess called. "I'm in the kitchen."

Dan entered the house, hurried past an overstuffed sofa and a wide rocking chair toward the door to the kitchen. Jessie stood at the counter with a sponge in her hand. Beautiful as always, damn it. "Where's Anna?"

"Hello, Dan. How are you?" She tossed the sponge into the sink and waited for a reply.

He halted. "Sorry." He grimaced. "Guess I've been in too much of a hurry all day to stop now."

"That's okay. Anna's outside with the kitten." She seemed to sense his concern and added, "It's safe, Dan. The yard's fenced." She waved toward the back door. "Look for yourself."

He relaxed, went over to the door and peered out the glass panel. Anna knelt in the middle of the tiny lawn, the kitten on her lap. "I wish that cat could stay outside all the time."

Jessie went over to the stove and stirred something in a pan. "Anna loves her, and the kitten doesn't seem to mind being hugged and carried around."

"I'll go get them."

Jessie rested the wooden spoon carefully on the rim of the pan and turned toward him. "Dan, wait a minute."

He stopped.

"I've made dinner," she said. "You're welcome to stay."

Jess made an enticing picture. In jeans and a long-sleeved cotton shirt, she looked like she belonged here. Except she was Jessie Carter, the star. And one of the most beautiful women he had ever seen.

He concentrated on her question. Something about dinner. The kitchen smelled good, like apples and cinnamon. "You cook?"

"Of course. Though I'm a little rusty," she admitted. "I'm making macaroni and cheese—nothing fancy, but I'd love the company."

He wouldn't mind a home-cooked meal, he told himself. It couldn't hurt to stay. Just for a meal. "All right," he agreed. "That sounds good. If you're sure it's not too much trouble."

"I'm sure. Have a seat." She shot him a happy smile and adjusted a dial on the stove. "Beer, wine or scotch?"

He unzipped his jacket and sat down at the table. "Beer, please."

"Coming up."

Jessie rummaged in the refrigerator, then plunked a glass and a can of Coors on the table. "Have you heard any news about Beth?" she asked as she sat down across from Dan.

"Not yet." He poured his beer and took a swallow. "I would think they'd be back soon, though."

"I hope so."

"Did everything go okay with Anna? I know she can be a handful."

"We had a good time. I was grateful for the company."

"I appreciate the help."

"Anytime, lawman."

He shook his head. "You're the only person who calls me that."

"Don't you like being a sheriff?"

Dan leaned back in his chair. "Yes. I like it a lot." He took another long swallow of the beer. "I gave up the county job after Wade died, but Gold City needed a sheriff and I like the work. I have a couple of young deputies who take care of drunks and car accidents. I do most of the paperwork and take the heat from the town council."

"You know everyone in town, don't you?"

"It's a good place to live. Skiing in the winter and fishing in the summer." He smiled. "You can't get much better than that."

"I guess not."

"Answer a question for me, Jessie. What happened when you got to Nashville?"

"Nothing too dramatic." She chuckled. "The closest I came to stardom was landing a job giving tours at the Hall of Fame museum." The buzzer sounded, and Jess jumped up and hurried to the stove. "The macaroni is cooked," she said. He watched as she drained the water from the pan and set it on the counter.

"Do you need help?"

"No, thanks."

Jess seemed to know what she was doing, he realized. He didn't know why he was so surprised that she knew her way around a kitchen. He watched as she assembled the casserole and put it in the oven, then filled the sink with soapy water and dropped the dirty pots in the water to soak.

"Then what? After the Hall of Fame?"

"Oh." She opened the refrigerator again. "I almost destroyed my voice because every day I had to yell to be heard above the crowd, so I went to a voice teacher for lessons. I was afraid I'd never sing again, but he taught me how to take care of myself. I landed a recording contract shortly afterward." Before she sat down again she poured herself a glass of white wine and peeked out the window.

"Anna is still talking to that kitten," she said when she joined him at the table. "Does she do that all the time?"

He was grateful for the change in subject. Maybe he didn't want to hear about her other life, after all. He preferred to think of her as a neighbor, not a Nashville recording artist. "Sometimes I think it's going to drive me crazy. Other times I'm glad she has a friend."

"Have the two of you always lived in the hotel?"

"Wade and Sue had a house on the other side of town, not too far from here. But I couldn't take care of a child and the business at the same time, so I moved us into the hotel, into the apartment on the third floor. Sue had lived there when she was single. She owned the hotel when she met my brother," he explained.

"It's a beautiful place."

"They put a lot of work in it."

"And now it's yours."

"It's Anna's. I'm just trying to keep it together for her, so she'll have something of her own when she grows up."

"She's a lucky girl."

He wanted to take her hand. Instead he gripped the cold glass. "We didn't always think so, did we?"

"No," Jessie agreed. "We didn't. But I don't feel sorry for her any more. I think she's the luckiest little girl in the world to have a father like you."

Dan met her steady gaze across the table. If she was Anna's birth mother, then she was one hell of an actress. If she wasn't, well, he'd spent some long nights worrying about nothing. He found it almost impossible to believe that Jessie would have abandoned the child. He had believed her that night; it was only afterward he'd questioned her story. "She's easy to love."

"She always was," Jessie agreed, taking a sip of her wine. "Does she like macaroni and cheese?"

"She eats anything," he declared, smiling a little. "It's a good thing I own a restaurant."

Jessie shot him a worried look. "A macaroni casserole isn't exactly fine dining."

"Sure it is," he assured her, wanting to see her smile again.

Anna opened the back door and burst into the kitchen, the kitten in her arms. A wide smile lit her face. "Daddy!"

He held out his arms and she rushed over for a kiss. The kitten yowled its objection at being squished against Dan's chest, so Anna backed up. "Did you and Jessie have a good afternoon?"

The child readjusted her grip on the squirming animal. "I beat her at Go Fish. And Simba played in her yard."

"Why don't you let him down before he scratches you?"

"He won't do that," Anna argued, but she bent down and set the cat on its four feet. Simba promptly rubbed himself against her ankles. "He likes me."

"I can see that." The cat was no dummy. Good food, warm milk and Anna's bed sure beat wandering around an alley.

"You and your father are staying for dinner," Jessie said. "So go wash your hands."

Anna left the room to do as she was told, leaving Dan free to watch Jessie set the table. If he didn't know better he'd think she'd lived here all her life. He'd think this was just another evening, typical of daily life.

He'd think...she was his.

Dan gulped and looked away as Jessie set a flowered plate on the table in front of him. He would be foolish to pretend that this could last, would be insane to even hope that Jessie would stay.

It would be suicide to fall in love with her again.

He continued to remind himself of that, as he ate the tangy macaroni and took seconds of salad and crispy bread. He listened as she told Anna a story about a horse that had tried to come on stage when Jess was performing at a county fair somewhere in Iowa. The food tempted him, the stories amused him, and the dessert finished him off.

He'd always had a sweet tooth.

When he'd finished the last of his coffee and Anna was snuggled with the kitten on the couch, both of them falling asleep under the warmth of a blanket, he thanked Jessie for taking care of Anna. He thanked her for dinner.

And he kissed her.

JESSIE SMILED to herself as she washed the last plate and rinsed it under the hot water pouring from the faucet. The dishes were stacked to dry in a wooden rack, the casserole dish held soapy water to soak overnight, and the pie plate contained the two remaining pieces of the best dessert she'd ever tasted.

She'd made it herself.

And Dan had eaten three pieces. With vanilla ice cream.

Jess sighed with satisfaction. This afternoon she'd managed to make dinner and dessert and take care of a busy four-year-old and her lively pet. She'd loved every minute. She'd been determined to make the most of her time away from the tour bus, so last week she'd borrowed cookbooks from Beth and pored over the recipes. Cooking dinner was a luxury she hadn't enjoyed in years.

Making love was another.

Jess dried her hands on the checked towel and tried to forget the expression in Dan's eyes when he'd looked at the pie, then looked up at her and smiled with such pleasure. She hadn't seen that smile since they'd lain naked together in his small bed, warming the cool sheets with the heat from their bodies. He'd smiled then, she remembered with startling clarity. And that smile had filled her with happiness.

He'd kissed her tonight, while the child slept. He had been about to say goodbye, and he'd stopped. He'd pulled her into his arms and touched his lips to hers and kissed her as if he'd been waiting for years.

She'd kissed him back, too. She'd kissed him with a startling pleasure that had slammed into every intimate part of her body. They'd clung to each other as if blizzard winds were trying to rip them apart. She'd wanted to run her hands under his sweater, feel his skin, touch his body. But she'd gripped his shoulders instead, praying she wouldn't make a fool of herself. Praying he wanted her as much as she wanted him.

And when they'd caught their breath, they'd separated, reluctantly. He'd stepped back, dropped his arms, turned away. Which was typical, after all, she knew. He would always be the one to turn away, and maybe that was for the best.

He'd bundled the sleepy child into her jacket and had gone out the door. He'd also left the damn cat on the couch.

Jess tossed the cloth onto the counter and peered out the window at the dark mountains. Faint stars dotted the sky high above Colorado, just as they had four years ago and a zillion years before that, she supposed.

But she was a different person. She was Jessie Carter now, with songs to write and concerts to give, with audiences to entertain and employees to pay. There was a manager and a fan club, a recording label and a bus with her name on it. She was no longer a starving musician, stranded and lonely, attracted to a kind man who had offered her shelter from the wind and snow. A man who took her with generous and eager passion.

Four years had changed everything, and there was no going back. All the kisses in the world couldn't change the past. It was time she accepted that and moved on. From now on, she would be friends with the lawman, maintain a casual relationship that would be safe.

No matter how much she wished it could be different.

"IT'S ONE HELL of a parking problem, Dan," Amos muttered, pouring an extra portion of cream in his coffee cup. "The town can't handle one more car, not with the tourists pouring in here to gamble."

"I'll talk to the city council again," Dan promised.

"They don't do anything. Just make promises to 'discuss a solution.'" Amos shook his head. "Damn fools probably don't realize that the Opera House has to have a parking lot."

"I'll talk to them," Dan repeated, taking a sip of his coffee. The stool beside him was empty. Was Jess going to show up this morning? He looked at his watch. She was late. She should have been here five minutes ago. If she didn't hurry, he'd have to eat listening to Amos gripe about how many cars came through town and kept him from parking in front of the café.

"You don't care, not really. You walk everywhere."

"True. But I care about traffic," Dan pointed out. "The town pays me to care."

"I guess," the old man grumbled, somewhat appeased. "You think Jessie's coming by this morning?"

"Doesn't she usually?"

"Yes, but she should be here by now." Amos drank more of his coffee and shot Dan a curious look. "Heard she took care of Annabelle yesterday."

"Yeah."

"Heard you had dinner there at her house."

Dan thanked Maizie as she put an omelet-covered plate in front of him. "So?"

Amos shrugged. "Just wonderin'. You're eating dinner there, she's taking care of your kid, and you're sav-

ing that seat next to you by glaring at every person that
stops behind it. Just wonderin' if something's going on,
that's all."

"Going on?" Dan reached for the salt and pepper.
"How could anything be going on between a country
sheriff and a Nashville star?"

"Well, I dunno. That's what I'm asking, Danny." He
leaned closer while Dan buttered his toast and tried to
ignore him. "Stranger things have happened."

Dan shrugged.

"She's a nice gal. Doesn't act like she's too big for the
rest of us. And you're what they call an 'eligible bachelor,' and not too bad looking at that."

Dan grinned. "Thanks, I think."

"Well, you have your advantages, like—"

"For God's sake, Amos! You're not going to start listing them, are you?"

The old man looked hurt, then settled back on his
stool as the waitress sped by. "Maizie, could I have a
refill?" Then he turned once more to Dan. "You'd better make your move, son. Take it from me, you're not
getting any younger."

"Thanks for the advice, Amos. I'll try to keep it in
mind."

He didn't intend to make any moves at all. Kissing
her that first night at the hotel had been a big mistake.
He'd told himself it hadn't been much of a kiss. He'd
told himself a lot of things. All of them lies.

He shouldn't have kissed her last night. Shouldn't
have held her against him and tasted the cinnamon on
her lips, shouldn't have parted her lips with his tongue
and kissed her deep and hard. Shouldn't have brought
back the memories of another night, another time.

But, damn. It had felt so good. And so right.

"Morning, lawman."

He would always know that voice. He turned as Jess slid onto the stool on his left. "Morning, Jess."

Amos tipped his hat. "You're late," he grumped.

"Sorry." She accepted a cup of coffee from Maizie. "I stopped in to see how Beth was doing. She has to stay in bed for a few weeks."

Dan had already talked to Grace this morning. "I heard. They're worried she's going to go into labor early."

Jess picked up her coffee cup and took a sip. "I told Grace I'd keep an eye on her."

Dan couldn't look away. She wore no makeup and her yellow hair was tied back in a lopsided ponytail, but she was still beautiful. Still very much the star. "Why?"

Her big gray eyes looked into his. "Why what?"

"Why are you getting involved?"

She blinked. "What kind of a question is that? I like Beth, I'm her neighbor and—"

"Temporarily," he felt it necessary to point out, even though the word irritated the hell out of him.

"Well, of course, temporarily," she snapped. "What difference does that make, as long as I can help?"

Jess had a point, he had to admit. He pushed away his half-eaten breakfast and concentrated on his coffee as Maizie took her order. Jess always ordered pancakes and orange juice, with a side of scrambled eggs. She was gaining a little weight, which was good.

"Well," she poked his arm. "Isn't that true?"

"Yeah, I guess." She would stay only as long as she wanted to stay, and he had to accept it.

"I was going to offer to take care of Anna, too."

"I don't know...."

"You think I'm not good enough?"

"That's not it." He would have asked Grace, but now, between her duties at the hotel and Beth's pregnancy problems, she wasn't going to have the time. "I'm going to have to find someone, but you taking care of her? That's damn awkward."

"Why?"

"What's the going rate for baby-sitters with recording contracts?"

She laughed. "They come pretty cheap. How about free, as a favor for friend?"

"And the kitten?"

Her lips curved in the most enticing smile. "Oh, that'll cost you, lawman. Big time."

His eyebrows rose. "Can I afford it?"

"I'll find some way you can make it up to me," she promised. "You have yourself a deal."

He took the hand she offered and shook it solemnly, despite the twinkle lighting her eyes. "I'll try to find someone to take Anna as soon as possible."

"There's no hurry," she said, taking her hand from his. "I like being with her, and one of these days I'm going to beat her at Go Fish. I'll pick her up Monday."

"She likes you, too." *And so do I, no matter how many times I tell myself how foolish I am.*

Amos cleared his throat. "If you two have settled your problems, could we talk about the parking spaces? Just what are you going to tell the council, Danny?"

Dan reluctantly turned away from the woman beside him and picked up his coffee, now barely lukewarm. "I'll tell them we need a parking lot, just like I do every month."

"Good." Amos slid off his stool and tossed four dollars on the counter. "Now I'll just head on home and start thinking about lunch, and you can get on with your courting."

"*Courting?*"

Amos winked at both of them and headed for the door.

"Dan?"

He had no choice but to turn towards Jess. "He likes to tease."

"I know. I'm getting used to it."

"He doesn't mean any harm."

"No," she agreed.

"Eggs are comin' up in a minute." Maizie gave her a plate full of pancakes and set the syrup pitcher between them.

"I'm glad to see you got your appetite back."

She poured maple syrup over the stack. "Don't tease. Lately I just can't seem to get enough food."

"Don't you eat in Nashville?"

"Nashville isn't the problem. Touring is. About a year ago, I guess, I just didn't feel like eating any more." She speared a bite of pancake and began to eat.

"It shows. You're too thin. And too pale."

"I know."

"Are you sick?"

She shook her head. "Not any more. Colorado is good for me."

*Then stay here.* Dan bit back the words before they rolled off his tongue.

Jess took a sip of orange juice, then continued, "I'm going to miss it."

He kept his voice neutral, his expression bland. "You're leaving soon, then?"

"No." She shot him another dazzling smile. "You

can't get rid of me that easily, lawman. I'll stay for a few months, until the music comes back."

"Until the music comes back?" he echoed. "What does that mean?"

Jess wouldn't tell him. Which annoyed the hell out of him and embarrassed her, too, from her dismayed expression. He was right; there were things she wasn't telling him. And he was damn well going to find out what they were.

"I CAN'T TELL YOU how much I appreciate this." Miss Jones, the young preschool teacher, hustled her tiny charges toward the braided rug. "Is this chair all right?"

"It's fine," Jessie assured her, taking a seat in the wooden chair that faced an array of expectant little faces. Anna waved; Jess smiled and waved back. She adjusted her old Gibson on her lap and strummed a couple of chords. When she was satisfied it was tuned properly, she looked at the now-quiet children and waited for her cue from the teacher.

"We are *so lucky* today," Miss Jones explained. "We have someone *very special* to sing for us. So I want you all to be on your best listening behavior, which means you must be *very quiet* while our special guest, Miss Carter, sings for us."

Twelve eager faces watched Jess strum the guitar. She didn't see Dan MacAdams slip inside and stand in a corner out of sight. Jessie sang, her voice sounding much too rough for her own satisfaction, but the children didn't appear to notice. Jess sang "Puff the Magic Dragon" and "We're Going to the Zoo," and taught the children the simple chorus. She sang for over twenty minutes, until even the most patient preschoolers squirmed on the braided rug.

She ended the concert with a rousing version of "Old MacDonald Had a Farm," with the children providing the required animal noises. It was definitely the oddest concert she had ever given, she decided, as the children clapped their tiny hands together enthusiastically.

Then she attempted to bundle up Anna for the walk home, although Miss Jones made it difficult by following her to the door to thank her over and over again.

Dan remained against the back wall, his leather jacket unzipped to reveal a white shirt and tie. He looked very much the sheriff this morning.

"What are you doing here?" she managed, as Anna threw herself against his legs for a hug.

"I came for the concert. I'm glad I didn't have to miss it."

"I didn't know you were coming." She hadn't known he'd stood behind her. She wished she'd known, wished she'd sung better.

She wished she could see him without making a fool of herself. They'd been deliberately polite to each other this past week, engaging in only the briefest conversations when he came to her house at five o'clock to pick up Anna. Every night he politely invited her to join them at the hotel for dinner, and every night she politely refused.

Every night she mentally kicked herself for being an idiot. And every morning, in the cold light of the Colorado dawn, she would remind herself that she was only a visitor. The handsome lawman deserved a woman who would warm his bed each night until they were old and gray.

"Anna told me you were singing today." He didn't add that hearing her sing was something he could never, ever miss. It was a temptation, unlike making love, that held no complicating consequences or emotional attachments. "I've come to take you to lunch," he said. "Since you always refuse to have dinner with me."

"I—"

"You can't refuse lunch," Dan stated, taking Anna's hand. "It's noon. You have to eat."

Anna tugged on his hand until she claimed his attention. "The Parlor?"

"Yes." He turned to Jessie. "Where's your coat? The wind's come up."

Jessie didn't move. "Don't you have to go arrest someone or something?"

"I've been to court in Granby this morning, and I don't have to be at the office for another hour or so." He took Jessie's jacket off the hook by the door. "This is yours, isn't it?"

"Yes." He held it while she slipped her arms through the sleeves, then she turned around to protest.

"Humor me," he pleaded, smiling down into her eyes. "I have another favor to ask you and I need to ease my conscience by feeding you first."

"Another favor? I don't understand."

He took Anna's hand and guided both of them out the door and down the steps. "The first favor was taking care of Anna until Beth is better."

"I offered," she protested, shivering against the sudden blast of wind that swept down the hill. "I love the company."

Anna giggled. "Simba loves you, too."

"He loves the catnip mouse I bought him," Jess pointed out. "And he likes to take naps on my couch."

"I do, too," Anna agreed. "Sometimes."

"I'm grateful," Dan said. "That's what I'm trying to say."

She didn't want his gratitude. "No problem," she muttered. "If you don't mind, I'll skip lunch. You can drop Anna off at the house whenever you're—"

He touched her arm, and frowned. "No. If you're waiting for me to apologize for the other evening, I'm not going to do it."

"I didn't—"

Dan didn't let her finish. He tightened his grip on her arm and ignored Anna's quizzical look as the three of them halted in the middle of the path. "I am *not* sorry, Jessie Carter. I'm not proud of myself, but I'm not sorry it happened, either. You can't avoid me forever."

So he thought she was avoiding him. She called it something else, like self-preservation. "I didn't want to avoid you."

"And I'm not sorry about what happened years ago, either."

"Neither am I." Her reply was so soft she didn't know if he'd heard her or not. But his fingers loosened on her arm and he took a deep breath.

"Then you'll have lunch with me?"

Jessie hesitated. She didn't want his casual friendship, either. She wanted him to look at her as Jessie Carter, the woman. Not the Nashville star with her own tour bus.

"Please," he urged.

"All right." She told herself it was because she didn't have anything better to do, not because he was hand-

some and sexy and kissed better than any man she had
ever known.

They climbed the hill, passed the Opera House and
the café, then crossed the street and continued for another block to Gold City's only pizza parlor. After the
three of them had ordered pizza and drinks, Jessie
leaned back and eyed the man across the table.
"What's the second favor, lawman?"

"It involves the Christmas concert." He cleared his
throat. "It's typically a fund-raiser for the restoration of
the Opera House and attracts people from all over the
mountain. Even Denver."

"And?" She had a feeling she knew what was coming next.

"I've been appointed to ask if you would be willing
to sing, December 22, at the Opera House."

"December," she repeated, mentally counting the
weeks until Christmas. So much for Jessie Carter, the
woman. "I don't know what to say."

Dan hid his disappointment well, she noticed, but he
avoided her gaze by giving Anna a quarter for the
video game in the corner of the room. She ran off, leaving them alone. "You want to tell me what's going
on?"

"What do you mean?"

"I mean," he repeated, leaning forward, "what
you're doing here. Why you're not on the road somewhere, performing. Why you're skinny as a stick, and
pale, too. What are you hiding from, Jessie?"

She opened her mouth to deny hiding from anything, but she couldn't speak the words to refute him.
"I told you, I needed the rest."

"It's more than that. Are you going to tell me, Jessie?"

She shook her head. "There's nothing to tell," she lied, sliding out of the booth. "I can't promise anything about the concert. But I'll think about it."

He put his hand out to stop her. "You don't have to leave."

"I just realized I left my guitar at the preschool."

"I'm sure Miss Jones will take care of it for you."

"No." She stepped back. "I need to get home. Just drop Anna off when you're through with lunch."

She hurried out the door and down the street. What on earth was the matter with her? When he got too close, she pulled away. When he kissed her, she wanted more. When he asked her a favor, she ran. When he asked her a question, she lied.

Jessie hunched her shoulders against the cold. The wind blew at her back, hurrying her along the path toward the preschool. She should leave Gold City, while her heart was still safe, while she still knew who she was and where she needed to go. She'd call Billy, tell him she was ready to come home, have him open up her condo and buy some groceries.

And when he asked her where the new songs were, she'd have to tell him there weren't any.

# 8

JESSIE DIALED the number and hung up before she could hear Billy's voice. What would she tell him, anyway? That she hadn't written a word that wasn't trite, boring and overdone? She almost laughed out loud. She wasn't as rested as she thought she was. A few weeks had fattened her up, but hadn't given her peace of mind. She'd attempted a few songs, but nothing had clicked, not a chord progression or a poem with any possibilities whatsoever.

The tiny knock on the back door came as no surprise. Anna would be disappointed about lunch, but she would make it up to her with a card game or a visit with Beth. They'd bake brownies and sing silly songs. She would pretend Anna was hers, then count the long, quiet hours until bedtime. Thank goodness Gold City had a library, however small. Mysteries and romances made the long evenings bearable.

"Come in!" Jessie hurried to the back door.

"I can't!" Anna yelled.

Jessie opened the door. The child stood there, the kitten in one hand and a small cardboard box in the other. "Pizza," she explained, holding out the box. "Daddy sent it to you."

"Where's Daddy now?"

"He went back to work." Anna stepped inside and

dropped the kitten carefully on the kitchen floor. "Where did you go?"

Jessie helped her unzip her jacket. "I left my guitar at your school."

"Oh." Anna threw her arms around Jessie's neck. "I love your songs!"

Jessie hugged her back as tightly as she dared. The tiny body in her arms was so very warm and so very fragile. "I'm glad, sweetheart."

"Daddy does, too." The child pulled back and grinned. "He plays your songs lots and lots."

"He does?"

"Uh-huh," Anna nodded. *"Lots,"* she repeated for emphasis.

Jess brushed the little girl's hair off her face. A smudge of tomato sauce stuck to her cheek. "I didn't know that."

"Knock, knock!" Beth waved through the window. She was smiling, her pixie face full of mischief. "Can I come in?"

"Of course." Jessie moved out of the doorway to let Beth enter the kitchen. "How are you feeling? Are you supposed to be out of bed?"

"I couldn't resist," Beth admitted. "I've been in that house for a week and I decided I had to have some fresh air and," she smiled down at Anna, "I needed a hug from my favorite little girl."

Anna giggled and threw herself into Beth's arms.

"Are you *sure* you're okay?"

Beth released the child and straightened. "The doctor said I could move around a little, but I can't climb stairs or get overtired."

Jess relented, pleased to have her neighbor's company again. "Then sit down and share this pizza with me."

"Ooh, that sounds good." She took off her coat and eased herself onto a kitchen chair. "Pizza Parlor, huh?" She eyed the box on the table. "My favorite."

"Daddy gave it to Jessie," Anna added. She pointed to Simba, curled up on the rug in front of the sink. "See my kitty?"

"He's quite beautiful," Beth said, then turned to Jessie with twinkling eyes. "Dan's bringing you lunch now? What does this mean?"

"It means he wanted to ask me to sing at the Christmas concert."

Beth clapped her hands together. "That's perfect! Are you going to?"

Jessie turned to Anna. "Why don't you take Simba into the living room and find his mouse?" Then she turned back to her friend. "I don't know."

"Oh, I hope so. It's beautiful at the Opera House. Everyone gets dressed up, and there are all sorts of parties before the performance. The whole town puts on quite a show. You'd love it." She looked down at her stomach. "I hope I'm able to go this year. I'd hate to miss it." She smiled at Jess. "You'd be a big hit."

"I'm not sure I'm going to still be here in December."

"I thought you rented the house until January."

"I did," Jessie admitted. "But I may have to leave early."

Beth's face fell. "Oh. I'd hoped—" She stopped and sighed.

"Hoped what?"

"You and Dan," she replied. "You know."

"I know what?"

Beth shrugged. "I guess I hoped the two of you

would get together. Anna needs a mother, Dan needs someone to love. Someone to love him. And there's something between the two of you, at least, that's what I thought. Mom, too."

"I'm not exactly the motherly type."

"Oh, no? You could have fooled me!" Beth helped herself to a piece of pizza. "Is there someone else, Jessie?"

"No. There used to be, but it didn't work out. Our careers got in the way." Funny, she wasn't bitter about Mick's rejection any longer. He'd done well, but he hadn't hit the charts as consistently as she had. The thought gave her some pleasure, although she didn't wish him any bad luck.

"And now?"

"Now there's no time for falling in love."

Beth chuckled. "Looks like you have all the time in the world now, Jessie."

"But it wouldn't be fair. I'm not a 'wife and mother' kind of person, Beth. Even if I wanted to be different, I don't think I could. My life is so different and crazy. Once I get myself back together again, I'll have to leave Gold City."

"Without giving Dan a chance?"

"He doesn't need a woman like me," Jessie stated, wishing it wasn't true. "We're friends, sort of. We have breakfast together at the café every morning and I take care of Anna in the afternoon, but that's all. Once I thought—" She stopped, realizing she'd said too much.

"Thought what?"

Jess remembered a snowy night and Dan Mac-Adams's passion. "I thought there was something special between us, something magic." She shook her head. "But I was wrong."

"'Colorado Snow,'" Beth murmured, her expression thoughtful. "You wrote that song about Dan, didn't you? He was the man who rescued the woman from the storm and took her in!"

"Yes."

"So it really happened?"

"Most of it, yes." Jessie wished she'd never started this conversation. "Want some more pizza? There's plenty here."

Beth put another piece on her plate. "Is he why you came to Colorado?"

"No, not really." At Beth's raised eyebrows, Jessie admitted, "Well, I wondered what happened to him. But I came for a rest. And inspiration."

"And have you found it?"

"No." Jessie rested her chin on her hands and eyed her friend as she finished another piece of pizza. "I think I need a piano more than I need a man." She grinned. "That would make a great song title, wouldn't it?"

Beth winked. "I know where you can find both. You interested?"

"Only in the piano."

IF SHE WANTED to torture him, she couldn't have picked a better way. Dan tossed his pencil across the room and watched as it hit the drapes and bounced to the floor. The faint tinkling of piano keys continued, up and down, high and low.

It wasn't the music. It was knowing Jessie was twenty feet away. He had only to get up from his desk, walk out the door and cross the lobby to the lounge.

And there'd she'd be, gold hair and blue jeans, making music.

He wished he could resist the music. He hoped to God she wouldn't sing, wouldn't even hum. He had no business falling for a hotshot country-western singer who'd had her picture in *People* magazine and her voice on the radio. He'd been insane to agree to let her use the piano. But it wasn't his piano; it belonged to the Opera House, and she'd offered a generous contribution to the renovation fund for the use of it.

How could he refuse?

Dan leaned forward and rested his head in his hands. What was she playing now? 'Amazing Grace'? He groaned out loud. Up until now he'd managed to control himself. Those kisses didn't count. They were accidents, slight mistakes in judgement.

She'd sung at the preschool, and he'd managed to keep from taking her in his arms. He'd taken her to lunch, instead. Or tried to, he amended, remembering her hasty departure.

But nothing could stop him from wanting her. Trouble was, she didn't want him. And never did. That one night they'd spent together hadn't meant much to her. She'd walked out the door, her footsteps crunching in the snow, and he'd never heard from her again, although he'd wondered if she would call or write. At least ask about the baby.

The music stopped. Dan took a deep breath, and then groaned as she started playing again.

"Used to be, when a man wanted a woman, he courted her until she said yes or no."

Dan turned to see Amos in the doorway, a grin splitting his lined face. "What the hell are you talking about?"

"The door was open," the old man explained.

"Of course it's open. I'm doing sheriff work in here today."

Amos walked into the room and sat down on the only chair. "Doesn't look like you're working too hard."

"What do you want, Amos?"

"I was going to chat a little about this parking lot situation, but now that I've seen you, I think you need my advice on personal issues."

Dan glared at him. "What about the parking lot, Amos? I talked to the council last night. They think it's a good idea. All we need is the money to buy Fred's land at the bottom of the hill."

"I'd rather talk about courtin'. You look like you're having trouble."

"I'm not 'courting,'" Dan replied. "I'm working." He waited for Amos to take the hint and leave, but the old man settled into his chair as if he was prepared to stay there the rest of the morning.

"You're in love," Amos announced. "I've been watching you every morning, mooning over your breakfast until *she* walks in. Downright pathetic."

They both knew who *she* was. "I don't—"

"'Course," Amos interrupted, "you're not much of a ladies' man. You're probably just out of practice."

"You don't have to make excuses for me. She's a big star, used to a lot more than Gold City and a small-town sheriff. She's famous, for God's sake! So just because I don't intend to make a fool of myself doesn't mean—"

"She looks at you like you set the sun."

That stopped him. "She does?"

"You haven't noticed?" Amos cackled with pleasure. "You're a bigger fool than I thought!"

Dan thought that one over. "A fool, huh?"

"Seems simple to me, son." Amos stood up and clapped the younger man on the shoulder. "You want the woman, you go after her. Maybe she needs a reason to stay. You ever think of that?"

No, he hadn't. Amos left as quietly as he'd come, leaving Dan to his own thoughts. *Maybe she needs a reason to stay.* Maybe that was true.

Maybe it was time he changed his tune.

FUNNY HOW IT CAME BACK. Her fingers were slower, of course, but as Jess played the familiar warm-up exercises, she felt the kinks begin to disappear. The piano, a baby grand, wasn't in bad condition. Someone had tuned it recently, and its tone was good, the pedals responsive, the action smooth.

Of course, the trouble wasn't the piano itself, but its location, smack-dab in the middle of the Gold Bar Hotel. The piano actually belonged to the Opera House, Amos had explained, but because of the renovations there it had been moved to the nearest place, which was next door. At Dan's.

She hoped she wasn't disturbing him. She ran through some of her favorite hymns, then switched to a couple of Willie Nelson tunes. She didn't play anything of her own, but promised herself tomorrow she'd run through the entire repertoire of Jessie Carter songs.

Billy wanted at least four new ballads and six footstompers for the new album. And she had until January to write them. If she didn't, well, she would have to sing someone else's songs for a change. Or Billy and Peach Tree Records would have to wait for new material. At this rate they would be waiting for a very long time.

Jessie looked up as Dan entered the dim lounge and made his way through the tables toward her. She forgot what she was playing and put her hands in her lap. She should apologize for her bad manners yesterday.

One of them was always apologizing.

He pulled up a stool from the bar and sat down near her. "How's the piano?"

"It's fine. Better than I expected." It was stupid to feel breathless, as if her lungs were being crushed together.

"Good."

That sat in silence for long moments, until Dan finally cleared his throat. "Can we start over, Jess?"

She clasped her hands together in her lap so he wouldn't see them trembling. "I think we've done that a few times already."

"Then let's try again," he urged.

"How?"

"I'm going to ask you to the Harvest Dinner, and you're going to say yes, then afterwards we're going to dance."

"A real date?"

"Yeah."

"I volunteered to wash dishes."

"I'll wait until you finish."

She couldn't help smiling. "That's nice of you."

"I'm a nice guy."

"I'm going back to Nashville," she warned, trying to be honest. "As soon as I write some songs and get my strength back."

He slipped off the stool and bent over her. He brushed his lips against hers until she reached for his shoulders. He deepened the kiss then, moving inside her mouth until she thought she would lose her breath. When he'd kissed her thoroughly, he pulled back and smiled.

"A lot can change in a few months," he told her. "I'll see you tonight."

"Tonight?"

"When I pick up Anna," he reminded her. "You're going to ask me in and I'm going to say yes and then we're going to open the bottle of wine I'm going to have with me."

"You have it all planned." Jess wondered if she would ever get her breath back. She hoped he'd kiss her again. Or maybe he shouldn't.

"Don't frown like that," he warned. "I'll think you're mad at me again."

"Go away," she muttered, but her eyes twinkled as she said the words.

Dan returned to his office. A stack of paperwork awaited him, but that didn't bother him at all. He'd finally decided what to do about Jessie Carter. He would admit he was attracted to her, he would treat her as he would any woman he was interested in, and when she left Gold City, he would wave goodbye and wish her well.

But he wouldn't let her get under his skin any longer. Avoiding her didn't make sense. Acting as if she was a casual acquaintance hadn't worked either. Maybe Amos was right, after all. Maybe Jessie wanted to stay, maybe Jessie wanted him. He doubted it, but he'd give it his best shot.

After all, he'd fallen in love with her four years ago. It was about time he did something about it.

JESSIE INVITED DAN inside and he brought a bottle of wine, just as he had promised. She'd concocted a beef stew; he uttered a token protest about staying for dinner, but she easily convinced him to stay. The stew had taken her two hours to prepare, and she'd stirred it for two more hours while it cooked on the stove. He wasn't going to leave without being impressed.

Anna chattered. Simba slept on the couch. Dan told stories about Gold City in the old days, stories he'd heard from the oldtimers themselves. Jess listened, fascinated by the town's violent history.

Anna fell asleep. Dan carried her to Jessie's bed, and Jess covered her with a blanket. Simba snuggled at the child's feet and purred quietly. Jess and Dan took their coffee into the living room and sat beside each other on the couch.

"Now it's your turn," Dan announced.

"My turn for what?"

"To tell me a story," he explained. "A story about why a famous lady comes to a small town in the mountains."

Jess rested her cup on the coffee table and snuggled into the corner of the couch. She looked at him as he watched her with an expectant expression on his handsome face. "All right," she said. "But it's not a very interesting story."

"Start," he ordered, never taking his gaze from her face.

Jessie took a deep breath and began. "During the last few months of the summer tour, I started making mistakes. Little ones at first, screwing up the words or the chords to songs I'd sung hundreds of times. Then big ones, like forgetting which song came next or when the set ended."

"Doesn't everyone make mistakes once in a while?"

"Sure. But not all of a sudden. And not without a reason."

"Did you see a doctor?"

"He said it was stress, that I needed rest." She shrugged. "There wasn't any time to rest. We were on the road, in the middle of the biggest tour we'd ever done."

"How does coming to Colorado fit in?"

"I started to lose weight. I couldn't eat, couldn't sleep. And then I started freezing up onstage. The first time it happened I thought I was having a stroke. I opened my mouth to sing the chorus of 'Fair Haired Boy' and nothing came out." She shuddered, remembering the humiliation, the fear. The band had kept playing, hoping she'd join in. Lester had stepped closer to the microphone and filled in the words, but the audience knew there was a problem.

Dan's voice was gentle. "Then what?"

"Every time I went out on the stage I was terrified it would happen again. And it did, three more times. Another doctor told me I was depressed. But that's not the worst."

"Good heavens, how much worse can it get?"

"I can't write another song. Not a note, not a word. Nothing," she repeated, shaking her head at the thought. "It's as if everything has frozen inside me."

"It's called exhaustion. You've been pushing too hard for too long," Dan growled. "It's a wonder you didn't have a complete breakdown."

"Maybe. The last doctor I saw told me not to worry about it, not to worry about anything. He said I needed a vacation and time away from the pressure of performing. So when the tour was over I came to Colorado."

Dan didn't look convinced. "Physically, nothing's wrong?"

"Nothing that time and rest can't cure. So I guess I have to take the doctor's word for it. My manager wanted me to come back to Nashville, where he could keep an eye on me, but I wanted a complete break. I remembered...Colorado."

"And are you feeling better?"

"I think so. I have my appetite back." She grinned. "You've probably noticed." His expression lightened, but he still look concerned. "And I'm sleeping again. Eight hours a night," she announced, hoping to see him smile.

He didn't. "You think something will happen if you sing at the Christmas concert? That's why you said no?"

"I didn't say I wouldn't. I just didn't know if I should say yes. What if I forget the words or the chords? I wouldn't have the band to back me up."

"It's that frightening?"

"Yes."

"Tell me something, Jessie. Do you *want* to sing at the concert?"

Jessie thought of saying goodbye to Dan and Anna, leaving Gold City, driving down the mountains toward Denver and the airport to spend Christmas with her band in Tennessee. "I think I'd like to do something to help the town. And if you think the concert would raise money..."

"Then say yes," he urged, taking her hand in his. "Stay until Christmas, or longer."

"I'll give it some thought."

"I have to know soon. We signed up a chorus from Denver and the local high school band." He smiled at her. "You'd be the main attraction, though, so we'd want plenty of time to get the word out."

"And if I say no?"

He shrugged. "You'll have to buy a ticket like everyone else. And I'll miss hearing 'Colorado Snow' sung in person."

"It's a special song," Jessie whispered. "With special memories attached."

"You wrote it about that night."

"It was a song that wrote itself," she admitted.

Dan slipped off the couch and went to where her Gibson stood in the corner. He brought it to her and waited until she took it.

She cradled the guitar under her arm and looked up at him. "You want me to sing it?"

He sat beside her on the couch and waited. "With all my heart."

She adjusted the strings until she was satisfied with the tuning, then played the introductory chords with sure fingers. The words and music to this piece were as ingrained in her as her own fingerprints; she had no reason to believe she would falter. So she sang her song of sudden passion and gratitude to the man who had inspired it, the man who had kept her safe from the Colorado snow and repaired her broken heart.

For when she'd arrived on Dan MacAdams' doorstep, she'd been a discouraged and lonely person, unsure about the future. Similar to how she'd felt driving through Colorado a few weeks ago, looking for the man who had put her back together and sent her on her way the next morning, into the bright sunlight after the storm.

God help her, she needed him to do that again.

He watched her as she played the final chorus, but she couldn't read the expression in his dark green eyes. Serious. Possibly a little surprised at the difference between the radio version and an old Gibson. When the final notes faded, Jessie looked up and waited for Dan to say something.

He swallowed hard. "Thank you."

She set the guitar on the floor, to lean against the couch. "It's not as good as—"

"Don't say anything." He held up his hand as if to ward off her words. "It was perfect. I've pictured—" He stopped and pulled her into his arms. His lips claimed hers, and she went into his embrace with a need of her own. She wanted to feel his lips and tongue twined with hers, she wanted his large hands on her skin, she wanted him inside her.

His hand was under her shirt, seeking her breast, when Anna called out. Her tiny cry stopped them. Dan ended the dizzying kiss and slowly removed his hand. Jessie adjusted her shirt as Dan climbed off the couch and left the room.

He returned with the sleepy child in his arms. "She woke up and didn't know where she was."

"Hi," Anna waved.

"Hi, sleepyhead. I think Daddy'd better take you home," Jessie said, feeling empty at the thought of spending the night in her bed alone.

"And Simba, too."

"I can't carry both of you," Dan grumbled.

"Simba can stay with me," Jessie told her. She gave Dan a quirky smile. "I could use the company tonight."

*Sorry* he mouthed silently. His gaze dropped to her lips for a moment, then he sighed.

After they left, bundled up against the chilly mountain air, Jess picked up her guitar and played a few chords of the Colorado song.

She'd rather be making love with Dan right now, but maybe it was best that they had been interrupted. She had no business being with him. She had no right to fall in love with him.

She hadn't told him the other thing she was afraid of. What would she do if she fell in love with him? When she left Gold City, she wanted no emotional entanglements, no teary goodbye scenes, no guilty regrets about what might have been.

She didn't want to take a broken heart with her.

# 9

DAN TIED HIS TIE for the third time and examined his reflection in the mirror. Not bad, he decided, giving the knot an extra yank. Good enough for Saturday night in Gold City. He left the bathroom and took his camel sports jacket from the closet. He hoped he looked presentable enough for Jessie. The dark brown pants were his best.

He'd give Anna a kiss, relay some final instructions to the baby-sitter, then walk across town to the Green Forest Inn. Jessie would be there early, she'd said, helping Grace assemble the cheese trays.

He smiled to himself at the thought of Jessie as a member of the appetizer committee.

"Bye, Daddy!" Anna waved from the couch, and Dan went over and kissed her cheek.

"Be good," he said. Then to the very young-looking teenager, the daughter of one of Grace's friends, he added, "Melissa, I left phone numbers on the refrigerator. Or call the deputy's office if you need to track me down in a hurry."

"You have a date tonight, Sheriff?" the girl asked.

"Yeah." He had a date with one of the most beautiful women in Colorado, a woman who kissed him as if he was the only man in the world she wanted to kiss. "Yeah," he repeated, "I have a date."

"Don't worry," she assured him. "Stay out as late as you want."

The child was giving him permission? He hid his amusement. "Thanks, Melissa. I intend to be late."

Dan grabbed his coat and hurried out the door and down the stairs. Yes, he intended to be late. He intended to sit beside Jessie at dinner and dance with her afterward. He intended to hold her in his arms until the music stopped, and then he intended to take her home....

"GO OUT THERE and mingle," Grace ordered. "You're finished in here." She wiped her hands on a paper towel and nodded toward a large tray of cheese and crackers. "And take those with you."

Jessie picked up the food and hesitated. "I can come back," she said.

"Don't you dare. Just put that out on one of the middle tables and then go find your date."

"How do you know I have a date?"

"Beth told me." Grace shooed her out of the bustling kitchen. "Now get out of here and go find that man of yours before someone else snags him."

"He's not my man," Jessie protested, but she did as she was told and carried the tray out to the huge banquet room. Wide windows faced the mountains, now growing dark as the last bit of sunlight evaporated from the sky. Three musicians had set up their instruments on a small stage in the corner. By the size of the amplifiers, Jess guessed they wouldn't be too loud. The room was filled with people, most of them gathered near the bar at one end of the room. She looked over the crowd, hoping to see the lawman waiting for her. She didn't recognize anyone. Maybe it had been a mistake to think she could attend a community function and fit in.

"Here, missie," Amos cautioned, appearing at her elbow. "Let me clear a path for you. Where are you going with that thing?"

"Somewhere in the middle of the room are some tables for appetizers," Jess said.

"Follow me."

He didn't have to tell her twice. People moved aside for him and Jess followed in his wake, weaving around linen-covered tables, across the dance floor and toward the bar. Amos cut through another cluster of people and stopped in front of a set of tables covered with appetizers. She set the tray on the remaining empty spot and thanked her escort.

"Nothin' to it," he said, grinning at her. "You know everyone here?"

She laughed. "No."

"Well, I promised a few people I'd introduce you." He lowered his voice. "Some are pretty shy about talking to you, you see."

"Oh." She'd noticed a few stares when she'd walked in, but Grace's friends in the kitchen had been friendly enough. She wished Beth could have come. At least she would have been able to count on her for conversation and introductions, especially since her date hadn't arrived yet. "Well," she said, pasting a smile on her face. "Take me to them."

"Not yet," a deep voice said.

Jess turned to see Dan standing beside her. Did the

man have to look so good in everything he wore? "Hi. I wondered if you were around here somewhere."

"Just got here a few minutes ago," he explained. "I saw you coming out of the kitchen, but I wasn't quick enough to help you with that tray." He smiled at Amos. "You beat me to it."

"Youth ain't everything, son." The old man winked, then turned to Jessie. "This kid your date tonight?"

"Yes." She couldn't help smiling. Suddenly she was having a truly wonderful time.

"Come on." Dan put his hand on her elbow and turned her around. "Let's get a drink." Dan's invitation included Amos, and the three of them headed toward the bar. Clusters of people greeted Amos and Dan, and smiled at Jessie as Dan introduced her. She recognized some of the faces from the café, and a couple of mothers who picked up their children at preschool. Dan handed her a glass of white wine while she answered questions about the music business and Nashville. She was aware of him as he stood beside her. The sleeve of his jacket brushed her arm every now and then, making her want to lean against him. She stood upright, as tall as she could be in one-inch heels.

"You look...different," Dan whispered near her ear. She turned to look up at him.

"Different?" She damn well better look different. She'd driven to Granby that morning to buy some clothes: more jeans and sweaters, and a couple of outfits suitable for dating the town sheriff, like tonight's slim black skirt that went to her calves and the matching knit top. She'd spent a small fortune on a gold necklace and earrings made by a Denver craftsman. Yes, she'd better look different. She'd worked hard enough at it.

Dan corrected himself, his dark eyes twinkling. "Beautiful," he said. "Very beautiful. I'm not used to seeing you in anything but jeans. You don't look anything like the woman who stumbled into the diner."

"I'm older and wiser now." *But not wise enough to stay away from the man who makes my knees turn to jelly and my heart beat faster.*

She didn't really feel older or wiser. She felt like the same woman of four years ago, a woman who had made love to a stranger, a man still grieving for his wife. And four years later, every time he kissed her she reacted with the same stunning passion as before. A few nights ago they'd both seemed to accept it.

Even welcome it.

Tonight was an official date. He would sit beside her at dinner. They would dance. He would walk her home. And she would, well, she didn't know what would happen next. He took her free hand and guided her carefully through the crowded room. They stopped often, as Dan seemed to know everyone in the room. He introduced her to his friends, his neighbors, his coworkers, and Jessie gave up trying to remember the names. Every once in a while a woman would eye her curiously, as if wondering what the relationship was between them.

And Jessie would lift her chin a little higher and smile. Let them wonder, she figured. Let them wonder as much as she did.

"I'M OUT OF PRACTICE, but determined." Dan stood by her chair and held out his hand as the band began to play a slow country waltz.

Jess stood up and placed her hand in his. "Is that supposed to be a warning or an apology?"

He chuckled and moved toward the dance floor. "Neither." He tucked her into his arms, his large hand firmly planted at her waist. "Just a statement of fact."

"I see." She moved with him to the steps of the waltz and found she could follow him easily. He tried no fancy steps, but kept her snug in his arms, against the warmth of his wide chest, as they moved around the dance floor. Jess sighed with contentment. She hadn't realized she'd been waiting for him to hold her in his arms. She'd dried a lot of dishes tonight, all the while hoping Dan would be waiting for her when she returned to the table.

He bent his lips to her ear. "What's the sigh for?"

"Contentment," she murmured, hoping the song would be a long one.

"Is that supposed to be a compliment?"

She smiled up at him. "Not really," she said. "Just a statement of fact."

"I'll take it as a compliment then," he said, pulling her closer.

She was sorry when the song ended, and left Dan's arms with reluctance. The next song was a two-step, and Dan swirled her back into his arms and led her in time to the music. Keeping track of the steps didn't leave much time for flirting.

SHE MANAGED TO FLIRT with him anyway. Through the speech made by the chairman of the town council,

Dan's arm rested on the back of her chair. Jess leaned back a little, to feel his arm across his shoulders. She bought raffle tickets, and won one of the many prizes donated by local business owners. To her embarrassment, she'd won a weekend for two at the Gold Bar Hotel.

When dance cards were distributed for the five official money-making dances, Dan bought all of Jessie's before she could buy all of his. They fought over the pencil. They smiled at each other as they danced one more waltz. And when the party ended, Dan helped Jess with her coat and took her hand as if he couldn't bear to be separated from her. They stepped outside into the cold night air and rounded the corner to the empty sidewalk. Jessie lifted her hand and felt the feather-light touch of something cold on her palm.

It was snowing.

"It's about time," Dan said, smiling down at her as snowflakes dusted his dark hair. "The ski resorts had to be getting nervous."

"I keep forgetting it's almost November."

"Yes," he said, dipping his head. "Me, too."

He kissed her, and his lips were warm against hers. Her hands crept around his waist to hold him close. It was as if they were simply continuing something that was started a few days ago, and interrupted by Anna's cry. His tongue teased hers, she tilted her head to deepen the kiss, and they moved as close together as the bulky clothing would allow.

She could have kissed him all night. She would have

stood under the falling, gentle snow and not known if it was November or July. She was that warm.

He lifted his mouth from hers at the same time Jess became conscious of the sound of voices around the corner. "I've waited all evening to do that," Dan said. He tucked her arm through the crook of his elbow and hurried her along the sidewalk, then down the hill. They walked in easy silence the rest of the way to her house, and she didn't have to invite him in. He kicked the snow off his boots, then came inside as if it was the most natural thing in the world to do. He followed her into the living room, watched as she switched on a corner lamp and shrugged off her coat. She draped her damp jacket over the back of a kitchen chair, then did the same for Dan's. *Very domestic, Jessie.*

Dan eyed the wood stove in the corner of the living room. "Want me to build a fire? If this turns into a storm you might be glad of the extra heat."

"Sure, if you don't mind." He was staying for awhile, then. Longer than it would take for his coat to dry, she hoped.

"No problem," he said, his expression unreadable.

"There's all kinds of wood on the back porch," she said, then hesitated by the refrigerator. "Do you want coffee or brandy or something else to drink?"

"Brandy," he said, opening the back door. He disappeared for a moment, but returned quickly, carrying the wood so it didn't touch his clothes. "To celebrate the first snow of the year."

"Good idea." Beth's grandmother didn't have brandy glasses, so Jessie poured the liquid into small juice glasses. She didn't think Dan would be fussy. He didn't seem like a fussy man. But then again, she reminded herself, she didn't know everything about him. But she'd known he liked brandy; he'd shared a bottle with her years before.

She carried the glasses into the living room and set them on the table near the couch while Dan knelt in front of the opened stove. Jessie sat down on the sofa, slipped off her damp shoes, and tucked her feet beneath her for warmth.

There was something comforting about watching a man build a fire, she decided. Dan crumpled up newspaper, arranged kindling and larger chunks of wood until he was satisfied with the structure. Then he lit a match to the paper and watched as the fire roared to life. He made it look easy.

But he was Dan MacAdams, a man who plucked strangers from storms and nieces from tragedy. He ran hotels and towns with equal ease, so keeping a house warm was child's play. Jessie was impressed. And very afraid she was falling in love.

"That should be a good start for you," he said as he shut the door and secured the handle.

"Thanks. I appreciate it." Her heart lurched as he turned around and smiled at her. Perhaps she was in love with him already. Or had never stopped loving him since that night four years before.

Dan sat beside her and picked up the other glass. "Do you know we've never been alone before?" He took a swallow of the brandy. "You had Anna when we met, and I've had Anna since you came to town."

"It's a good thing she has you."

He ignored the compliment. "You're the person who saved her life," he pointed out.

"I don't think her mother meant her any harm. Not really. I don't know what would make a woman abandon her own baby, but I have to believe that the hitchhiker knew I would take care of the baby somehow."

"And you did." His smile was wry. "I'll never forget the way you looked when you walked into the diner that night. I thought you were crazy to take a child into the storm."

"I was," Jessie agreed. "And I was scared to death, too."

"It didn't show."

She laughed. "Oh, yes, it did!"

"Well," he conceded. "Maybe a little."

Jessie's expression grew serious. "I'm not her real mother, Dan. Do you believe me?"

He cleared his throat and set his half-empty glass on the table. "Yes, I believe you. And I owe you an apology. I did some checking around. An old friend from the state police turned up some interesting possibilities. There was a hitchhiker, a young woman, murdered near the Nebraska border two weeks after you appeared at the café. The state police also uncovered a body near Berthoud Pass in the spring. Also a young woman, but this was a drug overdose, nothing more. Either one could have been Anna's mother, I suppose. I didn't pursue it. I didn't think it mattered."

"It might matter to Anna someday."

"And if it does," he stated firmly, "I'll help her find out whatever she needs to know. But the answers don't affect her life now."

"No." Jessie looked at the strong, determined man near her. "She has everything she needs. She's a happy girl."

"Yeah. And tonight she has a happy father. I'm glad we got to dance."

"Me, too. Take your boots off. Your feet must be freezing."

He grinned. "Out west that's one hell of an invitation."

"An invitation? For what?"

"For staying...awhile."

"Take off your boots and we'll talk."

"I don't intend to talk. Why don't you sing instead?"

She shook her head. "Not tonight. Not now."

Dan looked disappointed. "Why not?"

"Because when you kiss me I forget all the words to all the songs I ever knew."

His expression softened as he reached for her. "You're putting me in a very awkward position, lady. That's one hell of a choice—making love to you or hearing you sing."

"You can have both, lawman," she whispered as his mouth neared hers.

"Tell me how."

"Kiss me first."

He did, taking her lips in a searing kiss. He pulled her to her knees and held her tightly against him. And Jessie folded her arms around his neck as if she would never let him go.

Dan didn't resist. He wanted her lips touching his, her breasts against his chest, her fingers curled into his hair. He remembered how soft her skin had felt against his, how sweetly her body had welcomed him. How much he'd needed her warmth and her love. It shocked him to realize he still did.

It was useless to fight it; he'd given up days before. And if she didn't taste so damn good he might have been able to exercise some control.

But he'd been waiting four years to be inside of her again.

Four years of wondering where she was and what she was doing.

Four years wondering if she ever thought about him.

He'd spent too many hours playing that damn song about the storm and hoping things had worked out for her.

"I'm through waiting," he told her. He didn't know if she would pull away. She knew damn well what he meant.

"Through waiting for songs or through waiting for kisses?" She nibbled at his lower lip and then kissed the corner of his mouth.

He groaned. "I'm through waiting to make love to you, Jess."

"No one's asking you to wait," she teased. "Didn't you just say we were alone?"

He cupped his large hands on either side of her face and gazed into those steady gray eyes. Yellow curls spilled over his fingers as she looked up at him. "Jessie..." He stopped, having no words to explain how he felt.

"Don't say anything," Jess begged. She reached up and took his hands in hers and brushed them against her cheek. "All that matters is that we've found each other again."

And would lose each other, too? he wondered, but he didn't say the words aloud. Instead he touched his lips to hers in soft, silent agreement. Perhaps, for now, for tonight, it was enough to be with her again.

His fingers moved to the row of tiny gold buttons between her breasts. She reached for his tie, but he moved her hands away. "No," he whispered. "I've wondered what it would be like to undress you. Sit still."

So Jess sat quietly on her haunches and suffered exquisite, wonderful torture as he slowly unfastened the buttons, slid one warm hand inside the fabric to cradle her right breast, and kissed a trail of tiny caresses along the side of her neck. He returned to the buttons, and took his time popping them from the holes, until he separated the black shirt and revealed her black lace bra.

"You're as beautiful as I remembered," he said. "I've never forgotten anything about that night."

"I didn't either."

"I didn't get to undress you," he said, almost apologetically. He bent to kiss one lace-covered nipple, and the shivers that radiated from his touch made it difficult for Jess to speak. "You wore a nightgown," he continued as he unfastened the clasp between her breasts. He smoothed the straps from her arms and tossed the scrap of lace aside. "With pink flowers on it, and a lace collar."

His lips sought the pebbled peak of her nipple, his hands went around her bare waist. Jess steadied herself by grasping his shoulders. "You said, 'Come to bed, Jessie Carter,'" she reminded him. He wasn't the only one who remembered details of that night.

Dan lifted his head. "I'm a brilliant man. I think I'll say it again." He moved off the couch to stand in front of her. He held out his hands and Jessie, missing him from the second he withdrew, put her hands in his and allowed him to tug her to her feet.

"Come to bed, Jessie Carter," he repeated, a smile lifting one side of his mouth. His eyes were dark and tender as he waited for her to move with him toward the bedroom.

"Yes." She was half-naked and fully aroused, and she didn't want to wait any longer to make love with him. She wanted to remove that damn tie and rain kisses on his throat and chest. She wanted to run her fingertips along the smooth skin of his back, she wanted to feel the indentation of his spine and the sharp angles of his shoulder blades.

"Jessie?" He studied her, wondering at her hesitation, then pulled her into his arms. Her breasts flattened against his crisp cotton shirt as he held her against him, his chin resting on her hair. "Oh, Jess, I want you so much."

She wanted him, too. "Do I undo your tie now?"

"No." His chest rumbled against her ear.

"No?" Jess tilted her head and looked up at him.

"Come to bed," he ordered. "Now."

"Okay, lawman." She stepped away from the comforting bulk of his body and let him lead her into her little bedroom.

It was an old lady's room, with violets sprinkled on

the wallpaper and the matching bedspread. Grace had gladly loaned the linens, happy to have them used instead of growing moldy up in the attic. Dan didn't seem to notice the mahogany dressers with lace doilies, or the frilly curtains hiding thick white shades. He threw back the flowered bedspread, sat down and pulled Jessie between his knees. He was on eye level with her breasts, but his hands tugged her skirt off her hips and let it slip to the floor. Her stockings and silky black panties followed, and Jess reached up and unfastened the thick gold necklace. She dropped it to the floor as Dan's hands circled her waist, as his lips tickled her abdomen and his tongue dipped into her navel with tantalizing slowness.

He held her still while his mouth dipped lower, past silky curls to the soft folds of skin between her thighs. He pulled her closer, tasting her body and bringing her perilously close to orgasm. Jessie trembled as sensation, hot and strong, streaked through her, demanding release. But he lifted his mouth and smoothed his palms over the swell of her buttocks, then moved his hands back to her waist. When he lifted her onto the mattress, she made no protest. She was grateful her shaking legs didn't have to support her any longer.

Dan tossed off his clothes and joined her on the soft, aged sheets. His body was as warm as if he'd been roasting by the wood stove. When he slipped the condom on and would have taken her, she stopped him. Instead she rolled him onto his back.

"My turn," she demanded softly. She kissed her way along his furred chest. He groaned as she licked the flat male nipples and held his breath as she moved lower, to take him into her hand and then into her mouth. She explored the shape of him with her tongue, until he grew even larger. Until he urged her up, until she moved above him and, gasping for control, he entered her with deliberate slowness.

She felt every inch of him fill her. He gripped her hips and lifted her easily, holding her steady for his thrusts. The passion wasn't a surprise, but the strength that controlled it was. Jessie leaned over him and he nuzzled her breasts, stretching the nipples with his teeth until she groaned with pleasure. Something deep within her knew she had found a part of herself she thought she'd lost.

He moved faster and harder inside of her, enhancing her pleasure with every stroke, drawing every last wave of sensation from her until she tightened around him. Until she closed her eyes and the deep contractions of her climax radiated within her. Dan thrust harder and deeper, until he groaned with his own release. His fingers dug into her buttocks to hold her in place above him and then, after a long moment, released their grip. Jessie sank onto his chest as he wrapped his arms around her waist. The comforting sound of his rapid heartbeat echoed hers and his skin was warm where her cheek rested.

She took a deep breath and clung to him. God help her, she had fallen in love with Dan MacAdams. She'd fallen in love with the one man she couldn't have, the one man who remained unforgettable, no matter where she traveled or what she accomplished.

The lawman would always want more than she could give, but Jessie knew she could give him something tonight. She could give him all of her love, her kisses, her caresses. She would share her body and hide her heart. Because if he knew she loved him he would never let her go.

And she wasn't sure she could leave.

DAN KNEW he had to leave. As much as he wanted to stay until morning, as much as he wished he could come inside her again, he was a father with a baby-sitter waiting for him to return. He had to leave, if only he could force himself away from the warm bed and the willing woman inside of it. If he could extricate himself from Jessie's bed without waking her. Her soft hair lay tangled against his arm, her forehead was pressed against his shoulder. She lay appealingly na-ked; one breast peeked out from the purple blanket, tempting him to stay an hour longer.

Dan swallowed and looked away from all that soft skin. He eased himself from the bed and watched as Jessie nestled into the dent he'd left in the pillow. He pulled the blankets to her shoulder and resisted kissing her goodbye.

If she opened her eyes and smiled at him, he would make love to her again. Unless, he worried, she woke up regretting what had happened between them. Dan frowned as he picked up his clothes and tiptoed out of the room. He hadn't thought that she'd regret it, but he didn't know much about women.

He shut the bedroom door behind him and dressed quickly in the living room. It was almost midnight and still snowing, but not hard. Just enough to look good and cover the frozen ground, enough to make the sidewalks slick and dangerous. Dan tossed a couple of logs into the wood stove and adjusted the damper before searching for the rest of his belongings.

She'd told him to take his boots off; they were there in front of the couch, half-hidden under the coffee table. His jacket was draped over a chair, gloves shoved in the pockets for safekeeping. He put on his gloves and crammed his tie in a pocket instead. He wouldn't have to dress up again until the Christmas concert.

Maybe Jess would be here. Maybe she wouldn't.

Whatever happened, he realized, would be up to him. Could he convince her that she would be happy here? Could he replace the applause and the record deals with motherhood and great sex?

Dan opened and shut the front door with very little sound. He made his way down the steps to the quiet street and headed up the hill toward home. Tomorrow he'd call her. Tomorrow he'd start doing his damndest to make her stay.

Because if she left him again he didn't know if he would ever be the same.

# 10

"JESS? IT'S DAN. How about if I pick you up for breakfast in an hour?"

Jessie snuggled under the blankets and yawned, the phone tucked against her ear. She'd answered it automatically, groping to find the receiver so she could stop the ringing.

"Jessie?" Dan sounded amused. "Are you awake?"

"Not really," she murmured. "What time is it?"

"Ten o'clock. I thought you were a morning person."

"Not after last night," she replied without thinking, and heard him chuckle. "Is it still snowing?"

"Open those purple curtains and look for yourself."

Jessie struggled to open her eyes, but it wasn't an easy accomplishment. The shades kept the room dark. "Are you sure it's really ten o'clock, not six?"

"I'm sure."

"What time did you leave last night?"

"Midnight."

Jessie moved to a sitting position. There were parts of her that were decidedly sore. They had made love twice before she'd fallen asleep in his arms. "You sound awfully wide awake."

"Anna stuck a puppet in my face at seven."

"Ouch."

"Yeah."

Jess was too sleepy to be careful, too comfortable to watch her words. "I wish you were here," she said, longing to snuggle against him. Longing to do more than snuggle.

There was a long pause. Finally he spoke, his voice deep. "I do, too."

Neither one spoke for a moment. Dan filled in the silence. "Will you have breakfast with us? The hotel serves a Sunday brunch I think you'd like."

"Sounds great." If Dan MacAdams was beside her, she'd enjoy a hard-boiled egg and a glass of water.

"I'll pick you up."

"No. I'll walk."

"You sure?"

"Yes." She enjoyed the fresh air, and if there was snow, that was even better. It would give her a chance to clear her head of thoughts of dancing the two-step and Dan sharing her bed. "I'll be there at eleven-thirty."

"I'll save you some coffee," he promised, before hanging up.

Jessie stretched across the bed to replace the receiver, but she didn't get out of it right away. She wanted to spend a few minutes luxuriating in bed, a warm bed that held the faint smell of minty aftershave and the satisfying traces of last night's lovemaking. She would get up in a minute. She would check the wood stove and have a shower. She would dress in something warm and presentable, and then she would walk up the hill and try very hard to not to look like a woman in love.

It was not going to be easy.

"COME ON UPSTAIRS for awhile," Dan said, pushing back his chair. "I'm off duty today, and Jeff is taking care of anything that comes up here."

"All right." Jessie tossed her napkin on the table and scooted her chair away from the table. She'd tried a little bit of everything, from scrambled eggs to roast beef. The chocolate cake had been the final extravagance, though.

"But the piano," Anna protested. Dan wiped a smudge of chocolate from her cheek.

"What about it?"

"I promised I'd play her a song," Jessie explained. "Would you mind?"

"Of course not." He guided both of them toward the crowded lobby. Obviously the hotel's Sunday brunch was popular with the citizens of Gold City.

"It won't disturb the customers?"

"The bar is closed until this evening. Besides, I don't think anyone coming through here would complain about hearing you play. I know I wouldn't."

She and Anna followed him across the lobby, waited a moment while he talked to the lanky desk clerk, then went into the dark lounge. Dan switched on a corner light, enough to illuminate most of the keyboard while Jess sat down on the bench and lifted the lid. She helped Anna up to sit beside her, then ran her fingers along the keys to warm up. Dan sat on one of the stools along the bar to watch.

"I've appreciated being able to practice," she told him. She didn't explain that she'd found her morning hours at the piano frustrating beyond belief. While having access to a decent instrument was a luxury she hadn't expected, it was torture trying to write songs and coming up blank. In fact, the attempts had left her craving a nap or a brisk walk. Both had been more enjoyable than sitting at the piano banging chords.

"Here's middle C," she told the child. "That's the very first thing you need to learn to play."

"*You* play," Anna begged, her eyes wide with delight.

Jess smiled to herself. The MacAdamses were always demanding she play music for them. "All right, young lady, I will," Jessie declared. "I'll play something I wrote a long time ago."

She played, but she didn't sing. Not until the room quietly filled with people. Dan asked for her latest hit, "Time and Again." So she agreed, willing to give what she could to please him.

He smiled, and her heart warmed as she turned back to the piano and the song. "Time and again," she sang, "you make me want you, time and again, you make me cry...."

She didn't mind the audience. In fact, she didn't realize how much she'd missed performing until she heard the applause following the song. They asked her for more, and she sang for them. The only request she pretended not to hear was "Colorado Snow," because she knew she couldn't play it for Dan in front of an audience who would knew a love song when they heard it and might recognize the lovers involved.

Anna climbed in her father's lap and nestled there, her head on his chest as he held her in his arms. And Jessie sang, pleased that the songs came easily, and that her fingers were limber and strong. She wasn't in the mood to sing anything too fast, but the audience that spilled into the lounge and hovered by the wide doorway didn't seem to mind. A snow-covered Sunday afternoon deserved something special, after all.

She didn't notice when Dan left, carrying the sleepy child in his arms. It wasn't until later, when her throat was dry and her shoulders stiff, that she realized how long she'd been playing. And realized Dan was no longer in the room. She accepted the applause, she accepted the thanks and the compliments, but she hurried upstairs to the third floor.

"I'm sorry," she said, when he opened the door. She didn't want to give him time to shut it in her face.

Instead he stepped back to let her enter the living room. "Sorry for what?"

"For singing so long. For attracting a crowd. We were supposed to spend the day together and I ended up giving a performance."

Dan put his hands on her shoulders. "You will always sing, Jessie. And you will always attract crowds, whether you intend to or not. I don't blame you for that."

"You don't?" Staggering relief swept through Jess, surprising her with its intensity. God knows, she didn't want to love him this much. She didn't want their time together spoiled by conflict and unhappiness.

"Of course not." His smile was rueful. "Although I prefer having you all to myself."

"You have me all to yourself now." She stood on her toes, wrapped her arms around his neck and kissed him. Dan slipped his hands under her sweater and caressed her breasts. "But Anna—" she protested.

"Is asleep." He unhooked her bra. "In her room." He unbuckled her belt. "With the door shut."

"She never takes naps."

"The baby-sitter let her stay up late last night." He led her across the living room toward his bedroom.

"I like that baby-sitter," Jess whispered as they passed Anna's closed door.

"I'm liking her more and more myself," Dan agreed, leading Jessie into the large room. He shut and locked the thick door, then took Jess in his arms once again.

"How much time do we have?" He gave her an odd look, so she explained, "I mean, do we take our clothes off or leave them on?"

"Take them off," he replied, flashing her a mischievous smile. "And I'll do my best."

She pulled her sweater over her head, he unzipped her black slacks and slipped his hand inside her underwear to caress the smooth skin of her abdomen before he slipped the silk down her thighs. She struggled with her boots; he tugged them off with great impatience. His brown sweater fell to the floor, along with his slacks and flannel shirt. When they were finally undressed, they dove into the bed, a passionate tangle of limbs and caresses.

He was gentle where she was tender; he eased his fingers inside her as his tongue sought to give her pleasure. She bit her lip, trying not to make a sound as waves of sensation washed over her and left her breathless.

He eased his large body above her and made love to her as if he'd never touched her before, as if the scent of her skin and the taste of her lips and the slick, tight warmth of her body were all new to him.

New, and exquisitely fascinating.

And when long shudders shook his body and he collapsed on top of her, Jessie blinked back tears. She didn't want to love him. She didn't want to miss him when she was anywhere but next to him.

THE BOX ARRIVED Wednesday afternoon, much to Jessie's delight and Anna's curiosity. Jessie grabbed a steak knife and ripped open the cardboard flaps.

"What is it?"

"A keyboard," Jessie explained, lifting it from the box. "It's like a piano, only smaller."

"Can you play it?"

"Sure. In just a minute I'll show you how it works." Jessie set the keyboard on the kitchen table and plugged it into the wall socket. "Press on a key."

Anna pressed one tiny finger on D, and the sound came out strong and true. She tried other notes, going faster and faster until Jessie stopped her.

"You have to be a little gentler than that," she told her. "I'll turn the volume down and you can try it again."

Anna climbed onto the chair and carefully pressed the keys. Jessie left her and poured herself a fresh cup of coffee. It seemed she'd found the perfect baby-sitter, but she'd asked Billy to send the keyboard so she could work.

For the first time in months she really felt like working. Scraps of songs had been floating inside her head for days; note progressions and bits of poetry competed for her attention. She'd avoided the hotel piano, unwilling for strangers to listen to her faltering attempts to write new music. Instead she'd waited for the keyboard and she'd taught herself how to make cinnamon rolls and sugar cookies. When Dan came she planned to invite him to dinner. A plump chicken was roasting in the oven with sweet potatoes and instant stuffing. If anyone had told her that she'd enjoy a vacation baby-sitting and cooking in a town of four hundred and ninety-eight people, she wouldn't have believed it.

Or maybe she would have done it sooner.

Jess returned to the keyboard and played "Chopsticks" for her fascinated little friend.

"Again," Anna demanded, her eyes twinkling.

"Okay. Watch." Jess played it over and over again, until the child could imitate it perfectly. "Very good," she told her, surprised that a four-year-old could sit still for so long. Jessie glanced at the clock when the phone rang. It was almost five; that was probably Dan telling her he was running late.

"Hello?"

"Did it arrive?"

The male drawl could only belong to Billy. "Yes, just a little while ago. Thanks for sending it."

"Does this mean you have some songs to send to me?"

"Maybe," she hedged.

"What's that in the background?"

"'Chopsticks.' I have company."

"Send him home and write me a hit."

He wasn't really kidding, Jessie knew. "I'll try."

"How are you feeling? Ready to get back to work?"

"Better. Much better, in fact. I've even gained some weight."

"Not too much, I hope."

"No," she fibbed. "Not too much."

"When are you coming back? I have something brewing with the Grand Ole Opry at Christmastime."

Dan appeared at the back door and Jessie waved him in. He was early, damn it. She didn't want to discuss business in front of him, didn't want her two worlds to come together. "I don't know."

"Did you hear what I said, Jessie. The *Opry?*"

"I heard you, Billy. Loud and clear. I just don't know about coming back so soon." She watched Dan kiss the top of Anna's head and bend over the keyboard to see what she was doing. But he was listening to every word she spoke into the phone.

There was a long silence from Nashville. "I'll be in touch," Billy said, sounding aggravated. "Send me what you write as soon as you can. The new guy over at Peach Tree has been on my poor ass this week. We'll need new pictures for the album cover and liner, too, you know."

"I know. Don't worry. I haven't gained three hundred pounds and I'll send you some material for the album as soon as I can."

Billy wouldn't let her go. "You said you'd be back at the end of the year."

Returning to Nashville was the last thing she wanted to discuss while Dan stood seven feet away. "We'll talk," she assured him. "I'll keep you posted."

"Okay. Guess I don't have any choice," he grumbled.

She motioned to Dan to take off his coat. He didn't. "Don't worry, Billy. Everything will be fine."

He grumbled again, then gave her news of the band and some industry gossip while Jessie caught Dan's attention and pointed to the stove. *Chicken,* she mouthed.

Dan nodded, but didn't unzip his jacket. She hoped he didn't have another meeting tonight. They hadn't had more than five minutes together since Sunday. "Billy, I have to go. There's a lot of static," she fibbed. "I can't hear you."

"Come back soon," he shouted, hurting her eardrums.

"'Bye," she returned, equally loud and trying not to laugh. She hung up the phone and turned to Dan. "Hi."

"Why were you shouting?" He opened his arms and she went into them. Cold radiated from his jacket.

"Bad connection," she murmured.

"Nashville?"

"Yes."

His arms tightened around her. "They want you back, don't they?"

"Yes."

"Are you going?"

"Not yet," she said, pulling away to look up at him. "Will you stay for dinner? I cooked a chicken."

Dan nodded. He liked her cooking, liked sitting in this warm kitchen with her. "Sure. I'd like that. Is that what you were trying to tell me?"

She laughed. "Yes. I didn't want you to leave before I'd asked you to stay."

He took off his jacket and hung it on the back of the chair. "We haven't seen much of each other since Sunday, have we? And it's my fault."

"You're a busy man."

"Too busy," he said. "Monday was a council meeting and Tuesday night Jeff couldn't work. Grace is taking tomorrow off to take Beth to the doctor again, and Friday I meet with the accountant about the hotel's books. And you haven't been in the café for breakfast."

"I decided to cut back on the blueberry pancakes," Jess said. "I'll join you tomorrow, though. Same time?"

"You can spend the night with me at the hotel and we can go together."

"It's tempting," she admitted.

"Then come home with me. I've missed you."

"Me, too." Jessie smiled at him. "All right. If you're sure it's all right with..." She nodded toward Anna.

"It will be fine."

"Beth told me she's ready to take care of her again."

"I know. Grace thinks it's crazy, and I agree."

"I think she needs the extra money," Jessie said. "Why don't you wait and hear what her doctor has to say? And don't forget, I'm right here in case of an emergency."

"Right here at the keyboard?"

"Absolutely." She shot him a smile and went over to the stove to check her dinner.

He found it hard to resist that smile. He found it hard to resist anything about her. He fought the irrational jealousy of Nashville and whoever she had talked to on the phone a few minutes ago. Whoever it was had wanted her to return, to leave Gold City behind, to bring her songs and her voice back to where she belonged.

He might have to let her go. After all, it was her life, her decision. But he wasn't going to let her go without a fight. She'd come into his life once before and he'd let her leave. In fact, in his stupidity and pride, he'd held the door open for her and ushered her out into the cold.

He glanced at Anna, intent once again on placing her pudgy fingers on the keys and making some four-year-old's version of music. "That's a nice song," he told her, and she lifted her head to smile at him. Jessie came over to stand behind the child and watch.

"Play that song I taught you," she said. "Your Daddy's a music lover. He'll appreciate it."

Anna put her fingers on the keys and banged out an altered version of "Chopsticks." At least Dan thought that's what it was.

"See?" Jessie looked over to him. "I can't believe she's learned that already. I think she has talent."

"You do?"

Jessie nodded and absently stroked Anna's hair as she spoke. "Absolutely. Can't you hear it?"

*Hear what?* He frowned, wondering if Jess was serious. Anna's pounding sounded like a four-year-old playing with a keyboard, nothing more. The two gray-eyed, blond-haired females in his life looked at him with identical expectant expressions.

"I certainly can," Dan answered, fibbing tactfully. "Play it again."

"IF WE WALK IN together, will everyone know?"

"Know what?"

"That we spent the night together."

"I don't think anyone in the café is thinking about our sex life, especially first thing in the morning."

Jessie still hesitated. She'd showered and fixed her hair, she'd put on light makeup and her favorite bronze lipstick. But her eyes twinkled and her lips were slightly swollen, both obvious to anyone who looked closely. "Maybe we should go in separately."

"No way. We'll walk Anna to school and then have breakfast. No one is going to say anything."

"But they'll think it."

Dan shrugged. "So? Let them think anything they want."

"You don't mind?"

"Mind that everyone thinks there's something going on? Of course not." He planted a quick kiss on her lips and returned to buttoning his shirt.

"But—"

"Let's go," he said, cutting off her words. "Anna will be late for school."

"All right." Jessie grabbed her purse and followed him into the living room where Anna sat on the floor petting Simba.

"If it will make you feel better," Dan said, helping Anna to her feet, "we can go down the back stairs and out the alley."

"The back way sounds good," Jess muttered.

"Come on. You worry too much." He held the door open for her. But there was something in his expression that made her wonder what on earth he was thinking.

AMOS REACHED for the pitcher of cream. "You decided yet?"

"Decided what, Amos?" Jessie sat beside Dan in a booth this morning, and Amos had elected to join them. He sat across from them and stirred his coffee.

"About the concert. Folks want to know, especially after you played the piano at the hotel last Sunday. Got 'em all revved up, you know."

"Really?" She glanced at Dan, who continued to eat his omelet and made no comment.

"Yep. I know Dan asked you once before, but as head of the publicity committee, I need to know real soon."

Dan finally spoke. "Jess doesn't know if she'll still be here in December, Amos. That's the holdup."

Amos frowned and picked up his coffee. "Well, when are you going to know?"

"I'll stay until Christmas," she decided and sensed Dan's surprise. She didn't look at him, but kept her gaze on the old man across the table. "And I'll sing at your concert."

"Hot damn!" Amos grinned.

"Why'd you change your mind?" Dan asked.

Good question. Would falling in love be a good reason? Jessie glanced toward him and hedged. "I'm not ready to leave yet."

"How many songs?" Amos wanted to know, so Jess turned her attention back to him.

"Is four enough?"

"Yep. We'll draw quite a crowd with your name on the program, you know."

"I'm glad I can help."

"Oh, you're gonna help, all right. By the time this is over we'll have enough money for that new sound system."

"Sheriff!" Maizie waved at him and pointed at the telephone receiver in her hand. "Phone for you!"

Dan excused himself and slid out of the booth. He was back in a few minutes, his expression serious. "I have to go," he said. He pulled his wallet from his jacket and dropped a ten-dollar bill on the table. "Something's come up."

Amos wouldn't let it go at that. "What's going on?"

Dan grabbed his jacket. "The house on Aspen Ridge has been broken into again. I have to go check it out myself."

The old man shook his head. "Damn shame for that place to be empty."

"What place?" Jessie asked.

Once again Amos supplied the answer. "Dan's house, the one he built up on the mountain."

"You still have it?"

Dan put his cowboy hat on his head and frowned down at her. "Yes."

"I didn't know that." *And what else don't I know about you, lawman?*

"No reason for you to, I guess. Look, I've—"

"Do you want company?" she asked him. "Or is this official business?"

He looked surprised that she'd want to go with him. "You can come," he said, "but I don't think—"

"Great." She scrambled out of the booth and grabbed her jacket. "'Bye, Amos!"

"Well, well," the old man drawled, reaching for his cup. "So *that's* the way it is."

Jessie winked at him and hurried to catch up with Dan. His long strides took him across a room faster than she could run. She didn't question why she wanted to see his house, the place he'd built for his wife, the home he'd turned away from after she died. She'd seen him in his brother's business, in his sister-in-law's apartment, and in Gus's simple cabin. But she'd never seen Dan MacAdams in a place of his own choosing. And she wouldn't miss it if she had to run behind him all the way.

"DON'T EXPECT MUCH," he said, putting the car in gear.

"I won't."

Dan drove in silence out of town, and up the mountain until he came to a gravel road on the right. They wound up the narrow road for a few minutes until he stopped in front of a chain barring the road. Dan left the engine running and got out of the car, released the chain and returned to the car. A No Trespassing sign hung from a post.

Huge trees lined the road that went deeper into the woods to a clearing. "There," he said, pointing to his right. "I told you, don't expect much."

A large two-story log home sat tucked into the mountainside, its front facing the valley below. A wide deck wrapped around the two sides that Jessie could see. She hopped out of the car to get a better look, and ended up hurrying to catch Dan as he walked up the slope to the front steps.

"Watch out. There's glass all over the place."

Jessie stopped when she reached the deck. The stunning view stretched for miles. Snow-topped mountains lay beyond a ridge of firs; roads snaked along the valley floor. "This is beautiful."

"Do you want to stay outside? It might be a good idea."

She turned. He had opened the thick wooden door and stood waiting for her. "No. I'll come with you."

He didn't look too pleased with the idea. "Well, be careful."

The inside of the house was freezing. The downstairs was one large room, with what Jessie guessed would be a living room running along the front where they stood. A staircase rose from the center of the house, and beyond it to the right was what used to be a dining area and a kitchen. To the left was the only partition Jessie could see. "What's over there?"

"Carol's office." He went over to the window. "Looks like they threw a rock in here. Probably kids wanting a place to party. It's happened before."

"If you'll give me a broom, I'll clean up some of this. We can get it done in no—"

"Forget it," he snapped.

"But..."

"It doesn't matter, Jessie." Dan turned away from her.

Jess stood looking at his broad back and didn't know what to say to help him. He didn't want her here, and he didn't want her to touch anything. "Then do you mind if I look around?"

"Go ahead. I'm going to check out back and see if anything was left lying around."

Jessie peeked into the office, surprised to see dust-covered cartons and an old desk chair. Whoever had broken into the house hadn't been interested in the contents of cardboard boxes. She turned and went up the stairs, shamelessly curious to see the rest of Dan's former home. A balcony faced the large windows in the living room, and a small hallway led to closed doors. Jessie opened one and stepped inside a large room. A king-size bed, covered with dusty sheets, sat against one wall. There were French doors, and Jess wiped the dirt from one of the panes and saw a balcony. A lounge chair, listing to one side, was the only piece of furniture occupying the small rectangle. Suddenly Jess felt very, very sad. Carol MacAdams must have loved this house, and now she was gone. A house that should have been filled with love and laughter was an empty shell, a target for vandals and teenagers looking for a place to party.

Jess peered into the other rooms, empty of all furnishings. She saw a dead mouse and lots of spiderwebs. There was no electricity, and Jess assumed the water was shut off, too. She hurried back downstairs, hating the eerie quiet of an abandoned house. The front door was open. Dan stood on the deck, his hands braced against the railing as he looked down to the valley.

Jessie didn't know what to say to him. She closed the door behind her, but he didn't turn around. So she stood beside him at the railing and waited and listened to the wind sweeping through the fir trees.

"I built this myself," Dan said after a long, long moment. "From a kit. We finished the inside by ourselves. It took years."

"It's beautiful. Have you thought of living here again?"

"No." The word brooked no argument. "The hotel is convenient."

But the house was only five or ten minutes from the hotel parking lot, Jessie realized. Dan MacAdams had turned his back on this house when his wife died. She could understand his not wanting to live in the house after that, but why did he let it sit empty? "What are you going to do with it? Sell it?"

"I've had offers."

"But?" she prompted.

"Let's get out of here," he said, his voice gruff. He turned away from the railing and locked the front door. "I'll have to send someone out here to fix this window."

"I can't believe someone would break into the sheriff's house."

"There are a lot of beer cans in the backyard. I'll find out who did it eventually."

"I hope so."

She took his gloved hand, even though he hadn't offered it. Jessie looked back over her shoulder at the empty house, its windows lit by the November sun. She shivered, and Dan put a comforting arm around her shoulder as they hurried to the car.

He'd mentioned the house to her the night they'd

first met. He'd told her about his wife, and how much he hated being alone. Maybe that was why the house stood empty. But he had Anna now, and her silly kitten. He could make a life for them in that house, could fill it with his friends and a family of his own.

What was he waiting for?

# 11

"JESSIE! Do you have a minute?"

Beth stood on her porch, a sweater tossed over her shoulders. Jessie couldn't believe the size of her. She hadn't seen her neighbor in a week and her abdomen looked as if it had doubled in size. Jessie left the path and went up the walk to Beth's house.

"Hi. How are you feeling?"

Beth smiled and patted her belly. "Like an elephant, but I haven't had any labor pains in weeks. We might just make it to January."

January. She'd be in Nashville then. "You'll have to have Mike call and let me know if you had a boy or a girl."

"I promise. Do you have time for a cup of tea? Or were you on your way somewhere important?"

Jessie looked at her watch. She'd planned to walk around town, a distance of two and a half miles, before picking up Anna, but tea and conversation with Beth sounded much more appealing. "I'm not doing anything that can't wait."

"Oh, good." Beth held open the front door. "I've been dying of loneliness lately. I miss talking to the other women when I pick Anna up at school, and I miss that child's company, too."

"I'm sorry I haven't been over more." Jessie entered

the warm house, so similar to her own but larger in scale. Bright and homey, with antique furniture, lace curtains and quilts draped over the couches, the place always made Jess feel like taking off her boots and settling in for days.

"I've heard music, so I figured you were busy. I wish I had something to do to make the time go faster."

"It must be hard having to rest all the time. Did the doctor say you could baby-sit again?"

Beth made a face. "Yes, but I'm not supposed to walk too far. I'm not supposed to exert myself."

Jessie followed her into the kitchen and leaned against the counter. Maybe it was time to start distancing herself from the child, before they became more attached to each other. Maybe it would be better for Anna to return to her old routine, with Beth. "I could pick up Anna at school," Jessie offered, keeping her voice casual. "I could deliver her to your door."

Beth turned the heat on under the kettle. "You'd do that?"

"Sure. I need the exercise. But I'll miss the little rascal. And her kitten." More than anyone would guess.

"I think you'll see both of them anyway. Dan will stop by your house after he gets Anna, I'm sure." She grinned. "He's been staying for dinner, hasn't he? Sit down and tell me *everything*."

Jessie sat. "Tell you everything about what?"

"Don't act ignorant, Jessie Carter. You and Dan. Dancing together at the Harvest Dinner." She plopped a teacup in front of Jess. "Brunch at the hotel. Taking care of Anna, dinners at your house. Mom even heard him whistling in his office Monday morning. What's going on?"

"I don't know, Beth." Then she took a deep breath. She wanted to confide in the young woman who'd become a friend. It would be so good to talk to someone, especially a person who knew Dan so well. "That's not true," she admitted. "I'm in love and it's the stupidest thing I've ever done."

"Why?" Beth poured the boiling water in the cups and then sat down. "What's wrong with falling in love with Dan? He's gorgeous and nice and sexy and you two make a great couple."

"I'm leaving after Christmas. I have to get back to work."

"Can't you come back as soon as you're finished?"

"No. There's a tour being planned now. I spend about two-thirds of my time on the road each year."

Beth whistled. "No wonder you looked so exhausted when you came here."

"I was in pretty bad shape," Jessie admitted. She would never let herself get into that kind of condition again.

"Does Dan know you're leaving?"

"Yes. He always has, but neither of us expected—" She stopped, before she could finish the sentence. Neither expected to fall in love, and that was the problem.

Beth's voice was kind. "You didn't expect to find him again. And you didn't expect to love him so much."

Jessie blinked back tears and reached for her teacup. "I didn't expect to be so happy. Or so miserable."

Beth didn't say anything for a moment. "How will you feel when you leave him?"

Jess couldn't bear thinking about it. "I love my work, and I love Dan. I never thought I'd have to choose between two kinds of happiness."

"You thought you'd have it all?"

"Yes." Jess tried to smile. "Pretty unrealistic, huh?"

"A little." Beth ran her hand over her large belly. "You have to give up some things to have others," she mused. "At least, that's what I think. I loved teaching, but I chose to take a few years off to raise my children. It's really tough without the second income, but I think it's going to be worth it. I guess you're the only one who can decide if staying with Dan is worth giving up your career. Or slowing down, or whatever it is you'd have to do."

"A singer has to be on the road. And that's all I've ever wanted since I was sixteen," Jessie explained. "My father thought I'd disgraced the family when I left for Nashville. He disowned me right then and there because I wouldn't stay and go to medical school."

"No offense, but I can't picture you as a doctor."

She grimaced. "I can't stand the sight of blood. I would have been terrible."

"What happened? With your father, I mean. He must have been proud when you succeeded."

Jessie shook her head. "He died last year. And he never forgave me for anything."

"He must have been a very hard man."

"The most stubborn man I've ever known," Jessie agreed. "I called him every month. He'd listen to me while I told him what was going on in my life, and then he'd say goodbye and hang up."

"Every month?"

"Yep. For years. Until I got a phone call from another doctor, an old family friend. I was playing the Warwick Musical Theatre in Rhode Island, and I had just finished the show. It was about one hundred degrees outside, and Billy—my manager—called me into the bus to tell me my father had died. Heart attack."

"I'm really sorry."

Jessie took a sip of tea and tried to erase the memory. "It's okay, Beth. Really."

"Thanksgiving is in two weeks. Mom is going to invite you to dinner, with Dan and Anna. Are you free? I mean, are you staying in town?"

"I don't have any relatives, if that's what you mean. I'm—was—an only child."

"I'm sorry."

"Me, too." Jessie took a deep breath and wished her friend didn't look so concerned. "But I would *love* to spend Thanksgiving with your family, if you don't think I'd be intruding."

"You won't be. You're living in Gram's house. That makes you a member of the family."

Jessie was only too happy to be convinced. "What can I bring?"

Beth considered the question. "How are your pies turning out?"

Jess chuckled, relieved to have the topic of conversation switch to food. "I've mastered apple, but anything else is iffy."

"Then bring a couple of apple pies and a big appetite."

THE NEXT TWO WEEKS passed quickly, in a haze of afternoon walks to the preschool, visits with Beth, evenings with Dan. Some mornings she joined him for breakfast at the café; some nights she spent at the hotel for magic hours of lovemaking. In between there was the music; Jessie spent hours at the keyboard, perfecting the songs she would send to Billy. Sometimes the snow fell, or the wind blew, or the sun peeked from the winter clouds to warm the earth for a few hours. Jessie baked and composed and sang, content with the shorter November days and the early evenings that brought Dan and Anna to her door for dinner and kisses. She didn't think about the future, didn't let herself worry about the new year and saying goodbye.

Dan didn't talk about the future either. He didn't ask her to stay, or assume that she would. The subject never came up, because both of them avoided it. It was better that way, Jess decided. Better to accept this for the love affair that it was, instead of trying to build a future from nights of passion. He'd invited her to go Christmas shopping in Denver after Thanksgiving, though. He planned to take Anna to see the decorations and Santa Claus.

Jessie thought that was a wonderful idea. Thanksgiving weekend was going to be something special, she knew. She started to make a list and offered to take her Jeep wagon, since there was more room for packages in the larger car.

"What smells so good?" Dan asked, the night before

Thanksgiving, when she called for him to come inside out of the cold. "Applesauce?"

"Apple pie," she told him, turning from the stove. "My contribution to the feast tomorrow." She looked past him, but didn't see Anna. "Where's Anna?"

"Spending the night with Beth and Mike. She's been invited to help get the baby's room ready."

"So we're alone?" Had Beth done this so she and Dan could spend more time together? She'd have to thank her in the morning.

He wiped a smudge of flour off her cheek and kissed her. "Yes, we're definitely alone," he stated, after he'd kissed her thoroughly. "We're alone until tomorrow morning, when I pick up Anna and take her home to get dressed for dinner. Then we'll pick you up and go to Grace's house."

"That's all very interesting, lawman, but what are we going to do tonight? I didn't make dinner." Sheet music lay jumbled around the keyboard on the kitchen table, while apple peelings and scraps of pie dough littered the counter.

"Well," Dan drawled, tucking a yellow curl behind her ear, "first we make love, then we go out to dinner. Then we come back here and go to bed."

"You're sleeping here?"

He smiled. "If you let me."

Dan looked determined and very appealing as he gazed down at her. He also looked like a man who knew exactly what he wanted. "Do I have a choice?"

"Do you want to waste a night alone?"

The buzzer sounded, and Jessie whirled around to the oven to peek at her pies. The crusts were golden, and juices bubbled from the slits on top and dripped on the oven floor. "They're ready, I think."

Dan peered in. "They're done. Take 'em out of the oven and let's go to bed."

Jessie placed each pie carefully on the counter. "You know, that's a good title for a song."

"I don't know about that, but it's sure as hell a good idea."

"I'm serious," Jessie insisted, groping for a pencil in the clutter on the table. "I want to write that down."

He nuzzled her neck and little chills bumped the sensitive skin. "Later. Haven't you written enough songs?"

"I'm stocking up." But she dropped the pencil back on the table and wrapped her arms around Dan's waist. Winter was coming all too soon. Christmas cards were on sale at the drugstore and Maizie had hung a wreath on the door of the café. Snow had fallen three times this past week and Anna was talking about Santa Claus. This lovely vacation was going to come to an end all too soon. Maybe if she closed her eyes and buried her face in Dan's chest she could pretend it never had to end.

"ARE WE CLOSE?"

"No, Anna." Jessie turned around for the hundredth time and attempted to appease the child in the back seat. "But I think we're getting closer."

Dan agreed. "It won't be long now. Pretty soon we'll see Santa Claus."

"'Kay," Anna said, leaning her head back on the seat.

Jessie turned to Dan. "She looks pale."

"Overtired from spending Thanksgiving with 'Grandma Grace,' I guess." He shot her a quick grin. "Maybe going to Denver this weekend wasn't such a good idea."

"She's been talking about Santa for weeks. I don't know if she could wait much longer."

"We'll be at the hotel by lunchtime," he promised. "She can have a nap there."

Jessie looked back to check on Anna. The child's eyes were closed, and her breathing was slow and even. "I think she's already taking one."

Dan reached over and took her hand. "Thanks for coming. I'm really glad you're here."

"Me, too." It was as if they were a family, heading to the city for a couple of days of shopping and fun. She had her list of people she wanted to buy gifts for and another list of toys that Anna had talked about, although she had a feeling the little girl would be happy as long as Santa brought Baby Big Tears, a fat doll that cried and talked on demand, and a pair of pink ballet slippers. She didn't know why Anna wanted ballet slippers, but Jess resolved to find them.

The traffic around the city wasn't too bad. Dan drove through downtown Denver to Brown Palace, a historic hotel with a reputation for old-fashioned service. Jessie was impressed. The lobby was magnificent, and the green and gold suite that Dan had reserved was elegant and charming. She could easily enough picture the place as home to cattle barons and the wheeler-dealers of the Old West.

Dan winked, as the bellhop left the room after carrying their bags inside. "Part of the advantages of being in the hotel business. One of the owners is a friend of mine."

Jessie peered into the bedroom that she and Dan would share. She'd stayed at some beautiful hotels in the past years, but this one appealed to her the most. Maybe because she wasn't alone in it, she mused. Anna returned from surveying "her" room and raised her arms to Dan to be picked up. He lifted her and she snuggled against him.

"Let's go find Santa," Dan said. "I have a lot to ask him."

Anna's eyes grew wide. "Like what?"

"I want a new fishing pole, a camper shell for my old red truck, and a new Barbie doll."

Anna giggled. "You're silly, Daddy."

"He sure is," Jessie agreed, sliding her purse onto her shoulder. "Whoever heard of asking Santa for a new fishing pole?"

"Come on, kid." Dan set her on the rug. "Let's go find us a store."

They found lots of stores, but no one had ever told Jessie that shopping with a four-year-old couldn't be called shopping. It was more like an endurance test, a barometer of how much patience and energy a person had, Jessie decided. The stores were too warm, the crowds overwhelming, and her feet hurt.

"Was this my idea?" Dan grumbled, threading through the crowd toward them. He held a bag that looked as if a Baby Big Tears could be hiding inside.

"Yes."

"You can shoot me when we get back home." He

looked down at his daughter clutching Jessie's hand. "Somebody's tired."

"*Two* somebodys." Jess smiled up at him. "Do we call it a day?"

"Yeah." He took her elbow and she clung to Anna's little hand and the shopping bags. "Come on. Let me take you away from all this."

Back at the hotel he ordered drinks to be sent up to the room while Jessie tucked Anna into bed for a nap before dinner.

When the drinks arrived, Jessie sank into a chair by the window and kicked off her leather boots. "What did you order?"

"Tea for you, beer for me, and a bottle of white wine for now or later."

"You're brilliant, lawman." Tea was exactly what she needed, and a glass of Chablis didn't sound too bad either.

"I thought we'd get dressed up and have dinner downstairs. I bought tickets to the Nutcracker Suite for tonight," Dan said, easing himself into the love seat across from her. "Do you think Anna will be able to go?"

"She'll be thrilled." Jessie glanced at her watch. It was only four-thirty, which allowed plenty of time for all three of them to recover.

"And what about you?"

Jessie picked up her teacup and took a sip. "I'll love it, too. My mother took me once, when I was eight. I've never forgotten it."

"It was Grace's idea," he admitted, a sheepish expression crossing his face.

Jessie smiled. "How many stores did it take to find that crying doll?"

"Three," he answered proudly. "Got her, too."

Jessie put her empty cup on the table and curled up in the chair. "Then you're doing just fine, lawman. Just fine." She let her head fall back on the chair and closed her eyes. She never noticed when Dan covered her with a blanket and left to turn on the football game in the bedroom. She woke an hour later, refreshed and cozy, with Anna standing in front of her.

"Santa was nice," the child said.

"Yes," Jessie agreed, snuggling into the blanket. "He is *very* nice."

DAN PLANTED A KISS on her neck and nuzzled the tender skin. His unshaven face was rough in the early morning.

"Ouch," she said, running her hands along his naked back. He'd made love to her thoroughly, in the dim light of daylight. Her body tingled, and she sighed with contentment. They'd gone to bed right after the Nutcracker performance had ended, all three of them tired from the long day.

And waking up with Dan was still a luxury she didn't take for granted.

"Sorry." He rolled to his side, taking her with him. "You sure this was all you wanted for Christmas?"

"It's a start," she drawled, teasing his lips with her finger. She liked the sleepy expression in his eyes. "A Grammy award would be nice, too."

His arms tightened around her, as if he thought she

was going to leave the bed. "I thought 'Colorado' won something."

"I won Best New Artist at the Country Music Awards the year that song was released." It had been a mistake to bring up the subject, she realized. He didn't want reminders of her life outside of Colorado any more than she did. She wished she had kept her big mouth shut. "What do you want to do today?"

"Stay here. Like this."

"No such luck, lawman. I have Christmas presents to buy."

"How about if I stay here this morning with Anna while you shop?"

An offer too good to be true, Jess thought. "There must be another football game on."

"Colorado State plays at eleven," he admitted. "I'll shop later. If not, I can always get anything else I need in Granby or Gold City."

"Can we do breakfast in bed?"

"We can do anything you want in bed."

Jessie eased away from him and reached for the phone on the nightstand. "You need to keep up your strength, lawman. How do you want your eggs?"

"In an omelet." He reached for and tugged her naked body to his. "But not right now."


"YOUR TURN," Jessie announced, arms loaded with packages. Dan stood dumbfounded as she turned sideways to get through the door.

"How much stuff did you buy?"

"Lots," she stated, satisfied with her morning. "Sorry I'm late."

"No problem." He took some of the bags from her and set them on the floor.

"Don't look in those green bags," she cautioned.

"Are those for me?"

She shrugged off her coat and hung it in the closet. "I'm not telling you a thing. No matter how much you beg."

He pretended to jostle the bags. "Give me a hint."

"Put those down!"

Anna looked up from her coloring book. "Did you see Santa again, Jessie?"

"I sure did."

"Was he nice?"

"Very nice," she assured her. "And he was very busy, too." She turned to Dan. "The stores were even more crowded than yesterday. Be prepared."

He gulped. "I don't have much to do."

"Take your time." Jessie went to the phone. "I'm going to order a sandwich and keep Anna company while she colors."

"I won't be long," he promised. "I'll probably just get some fresh air." He pulled his shopping list from his wallet and frowned. "Do you think Grace would like an espresso machine?"

ANNA STARTED VOMITING at three o'clock, half an hour after Dan had left. Jessie tried not to panic, but it wasn't easy. She wiped Anna's face and discovered her skin was hot to the touch. No wonder she'd been content to color and play with her dolls all morning. The child had been sick and neither she nor Dan had noticed.

"I don't feel good," Anna whimpered.

"I know. Try to sleep." Jessie tucked Anna into her bed and put a cool washcloth on her head, the two things she remembered her mother doing for her. She hoped Dan would return soon. He'd probably been through this before. He'd know what to do.

It was a long two hours. Anna threw up every twenty minutes, like clockwork, until Jess figured her poor little stomach must surely be empty. Jess sang songs to soothe the child, wiped her face with cool cloths and prayed that Dan would find an espresso machine quickly and return to the hotel. Calling a doctor would be a decision Dan should make, she decided. Unless things became worse.

Anna was asleep when Jess heard Dan unlock the door and she hoped he wouldn't call out her name. He appeared at the bedroom door, his smile of welcome turning to worry when he saw her face.

"What's the matter?" He hurried over to the bed.

"Shh," Jessie cautioned. "She's finally resting. She's been vomiting for hours."

His eyes went to the cloth on Anna's forehead. "Is she running a fever?"

"I think so, but I don't have a thermometer."

"I'm going to call a doctor." He picked up the phone and dialed the front desk.

"Mommy!" Anna struggled to sit up, frantic to find Jessie. *"Mommy!"*

Jessie ignored Dan's stunned expression. She gathered the little girl in her arms and reached for the towel at the same time. When Anna was through heaving, Jess held her until she stopped crying while Dan talked to the manager at the front desk about medical care.

He was pale when he hung up the phone. "They think we should take her to the hospital. It's probably just a flu bug, but there's a hospital nearby with a walk-in clinic, and hopefully someone there can tell us what's wrong."

"Good idea." She settled the child back onto the pillows. "Get her coat and we'll wrap her in a blanket, too."

He didn't move, instead he stared down at her with an odd expression on his face. "She called you Mommy."

Jessie climbed off the bed and tried to brush him aside. "Maybe it made her feel better. I think she might have been dreaming and—"

Dan didn't seem too impressed with the explanation. "But *Mommy?*"

"It's not that big a deal—"

He interrupted her. "It's not right, Jess. You know it isn't right."

She didn't care what was right or wrong at this point. She just wanted to get Anna to a doctor. "Will you *move?*"

Dan stepped back, but he looked as if he'd been slapped. "You're not her mother, Jess." His voice was quiet, but with a steely undercurrent. "You're a country singer trying to put your life back together, and you landed in Gold City. Temporarily."

"I've never pretended to be anything else," she whispered. She hurried to the closet for Anna's coat.

He raised his eyebrows. "You haven't?"

"I can't help what she called me today. I told you it

made her feel better. I think she's a little delirious and—"

"Let's go," he said, plucking Anna's coat from Jessie's hands. "You're right about one thing—we're wasting time."

"Dan."

He turned. "What?"

"I'm sorry."

"So am I." He looked past her to the child on the bed. "I love that child, Jessie. If anything ever happened to her, I—"

"She's going to be fine." Jess put her hand on his arm. "Really. We'll both make sure of it."

"You're right," he said, his voice heavy with worry and something else she couldn't identify. "She's going to be fine. No matter what I have to do to make sure of it, Anna's going to be fine."

# 12

JESSIE DOODLED on the sheet music, drawing sad faces inside the whole notes of the song she'd thought had such promise. She hadn't been able to concentrate on work since they'd returned to Gold City from Denver, since Dan had dropped her off in front of her house and hadn't called since.

Except once, to tell her that Anna was better, but he'd arranged for someone else to take the child to Beth's house after preschool. He said he didn't want to impose any longer.

*Impose.* She wrote the word at the top of the paper. She hadn't known one word could hurt so much.

She wrote another word down. *Mommy.* The word that had caused all the trouble. A sick child had called her mommy and her father had been terribly upset. So upset that he wouldn't speak to her, and kept the child away from her as if Jess would contaminate her.

Four days had passed since she'd seen him. It was not even ten o'clock and she'd drunk an entire pot of coffee and three cups of tea since she'd gotten up at five. Somehow sleep wasn't coming easily these past few nights.

She jumped when the phone rang. She let it ring twice before she picked it up. She wanted it to be Dan calling, with a smile in his voice, asking what she was cooking for dinner. Or explaining why he hadn't eaten breakfast at the café this week.

"Hello?"

Beth's voice greeted her. "Hi! What's up? Did I catch you in the middle of work?"

"Not really. How are you?"

"I'm okay, but I've missed your visits after pre-school. Sophia Johnson said she didn't know why you couldn't bring Anna here any more. Don't tell me you're leaving already."

"I'm not," Jessie assured her.

"Then come over and have tea with me. Tell me about your weekend and every skinny outfit you bought."

Jessie longed to sit at her friend's house and pour her heart out, but she didn't want anyone to know what a fool she had been. She didn't know what was going on, and until she talked to Dan, she wanted to pretend that he was just busy. "I can't."

"Okay. Maybe tomorrow?"

"Yes, maybe tomorrow."

"I heard you had a rough weekend." Beth's voice grew serious. "There's nothing worse than a child with the stomach flu."

"It was pretty scary, but the doctor at the hospital assured us that it wasn't anything serious."

"Dan must have been a wreck."

"Yes." Dan was a wreck, all right. He had rarely spoken to her after the scene in Anna's room. They had stayed one more night in the hotel, since Anna was too sick to drive home, and he'd slept on the floor by his daughter's bed. Just in case she needed him, he'd said.

"Did you come back Sunday? I thought I saw a light."

"Yes."

"It must have been fun to shop. I had to do everything by catalogue this year."

"I've done that, too. When I've been on the road." *Where I'll be in a few months.* Jessie broke the pencil in half.

"Are you sure you're all right, Jessie? You're not coming down with the flu, too, are you?"

"No. I think I'm just tired." *And heartbroken. And frightened. And very, very lonely for one particular man.* "Thanks for the invitation, though. I'll call you later on this week."

"You don't have to call," Beth said. "Just walk over anytime. Especially if you need to talk."

Jessie thanked her and hung up. She wanted to talk, but she wanted to talk to Dan. She'd give him one more day, then she'd hunt him down and find out exactly what was going on.

"Meow!"

Jessie, hunched over to pick up wood for the stove, paused to listen. A hungry cat somewhere nearby wanted attention.

"Meow!" it pleaded again, and Jessie put the wood back down on the porch and followed the sound of the crying cat to her back yard. On the other side of the fence, hidden by Beth's grandmother's raspberry bushes, Simba sat. When he saw her he opened his mouth and complained louder.

"Simba! What are you doing here?" Jessie went

through the gate and around the other side to scoop up the kitten. He was almost fully grown, but still too thin. He snuggled into her arms and began to purr as Jessie carried him into the house. When she set him on the floor he rubbed against her ankles and cried again, so she gave him a bowl of milk and the canned tuna she'd planned to have for lunch.

Simba shouldn't be roaming around town. Maybe she could return him before Anna missed him. She called Dan's apartment at the hotel, but there was no answer. Then she tried the main switchboard, hoping she'd find him. But Grace answered, and apologized for not knowing where her boss was.

"That's okay," Jessie said, hiding her disappointment. "It's just that Anna's cat showed up at my fence—"

"*What?* Oh, thank goodness!" Her voice faded as she spoke to someone else. "Jeff! Jessie found the cat!"

"Grace?"

"I'm here. You wouldn't believe how we've looked for that kitten. Dan let him out two days ago and he didn't come back. Anna has been in tears and I swear Dan must have searched all of Gold City looking for any signs of that cat."

Except near my house, Jessie thought with some bitterness. He couldn't come near here, for fear of...what? "What should I do with it? Take it to Beth's house?"

"Oh, no. She's allergic. I'll tell Dan. He's out on a call right now, but I don't know how long he'll be."

"Well, tell him the cat is here. He can pick him up whenever he wants." She thanked Grace once again for including her at Thanksgiving, then hung up and looked for the little troublemaker. He was sound asleep on the living room couch, curled into a ball and purring noisily. Anna must have been heartbroken over losing her kitten. Jessie looked at her watch. If she left now she could take Simba to the preschool and show Anna that he was safe. Then she would return the wandering cat to the hotel and have a few words with Dan.

He couldn't avoid her forever. She needed to see him, to try to make things right between them. It was December 1 already; before she knew it she'd be back in Nashville.

"HERE. I heard you were looking for this." Jessie handed Dan the cat.

He took it, cradling it awkwardly in his arms as he stood in the doorway of his apartment. "Grace told me the damn thing turned up in your yard. Anna is going to be thrilled. She's been crying for two nights over this animal."

"I wish you'd told me. I could have helped you look for it."

Dan didn't reply, so Jessie pretended she didn't notice his silence. "Well, anyway, I stopped by the preschool and showed her. I thought I'd better bring Simba home before he got into any more trouble." She waited for him to invite her in. He finally took the hint and stepped back to usher her inside, but he didn't look happy about it. "I fed him," Jess explained. "I think he must have been lost and finally found a place he recognized."

"I'll get him a leash. I'm not going through this

again." Dan tossed the cat into Anna's room and shut the door. "For now he stays in there."

Jessie stood by the couch, uncertain what to do next. Then she took a deep breath. "What's going on, Dan?"

"What do you mean?"

"Don't," she pleaded. "Don't pretend there isn't anything wrong. You've been avoiding me for days. And all because Anna called me mommy when she was sick. Is this the way it's going to end?"

Dan was in front of her in two quick strides. He took her face in his hands and bent down to touch her lips with his. The kiss was harsh and demanding, passionate and final. When he released her he backed up and looked down into her eyes. "Yes. This is *exactly* the way it's going to end."

Jessie stopped herself from going into his arms. She struggled to find her voice. "Are you sure?"

"I'm just trying to end this before we all get hurt."

She thought she could hear her heart breaking in half. "Maybe it's too late."

He shook his head. "I hope not, Jess. For all of our sakes."

"You've decided it's over? Just like that?"

"It was going to be over sooner or later. You're leaving soon. I tried to pretend that wasn't going to happen, but we both knew this was a short-term thing."

"I could come back. In between tours, I could—"

"No." His voice was harsh, the lines in his face etched deep. "I don't want a part-time lover, Jessie. I don't want to be wondering where you are, or when you'll find time to come back home. I want you here, with me, always."

"Is this some kind of ultimatum?"

"I don't know what to call it, Jess, but I know I don't want—" He stopped abruptly.

She finished the sentence for him. "You don't want a singer, some country songwriter who hauls guitars around for a living." Jessie couldn't hide her bitterness. "Isn't that what you were going to say?"

Dan didn't speak. He set his jaw tight and frowned.

Anger, hot and painful, shook Jessie to her toes. The need to retaliate overwhelmed her. "At least I have a life," she snapped. "I've made my own way, doing what made me happy. You, on the other hand, are living in your brother's apartment, with your sister-in-law's furniture." She waved her arms around the room. "You're raising their child and running their business. What happened to *your* life, Dan?"

"Shut up, Jessie. You don't know what you're talking about."

"You live here while your own house rots on the mountain and I don't know what I'm talking about?" Her voice quavered. "Sell it, burn it down, clean it up, but get on with your life, Dan."

He pointed to the door, his mouth forced into an angry line. "Get out."

"I will." She backed up a step. "But you could have come with me. You and Anna. We could have lived in Nashville, we could have traveled. We still could." She swallowed, her anger fading as she looked into his dark eyes. "We could make it work, if we wanted to spend our lives together." Her eyes filled with tears but she brushed them aside, hoping he hadn't noticed. She put her hand on the door and swung it open. "You never even told me you loved me, you know. I guess you don't."

He was silent. Finally he answered, "No, I guess I don't."

"It was just too much of a risk, wasn't it?" When he didn't answer, Jessie stepped into the hall. She looked back before she shut the door behind her. "It's too bad, you know? Because I love you, lawman. I love you a hell of a lot."

Jessie shut the door and didn't look back when she heard the door open. She knew he stood in the doorway; she could feel his gaze on the back of her neck. But she didn't turn around. If he wanted to stop her, all he had to do was call her name.

The hall stayed silent, except for the soft fall of Jessie's boots on the carpet. She hurried down the back staircase and out into the alley behind the building. She didn't know she was crying until her cheeks, damp with tears, burned in the harsh December wind.

It was time to go home.

"THIS ONE'S SURE to be a hit. It might be the album's title song." Billy shoved the sheet music across the wide meeting table. "What do you think?"

Jessie barely glanced at it. "Whatever you say."

"I booked the recording studio, and the backup is all set for Monday."

"Fine."

"We're not going to do it all at once, by the way." He picked up another folder and opened it. "Now this one needs work. It drags in the middle, and some of the lyrics need punching up. I think I'll have Davis come in and work on it."

"Fine."

Billy gave her a sharp glance. "You don't even know which one I'm talking about, do you?"

"'Heaven at Midnight,'" Jessie stated. "I had trouble with the middle. Right?"

"Yeah," he muttered. "Right." Billy shoved his tan cowboy hat from his forehead and leaned back in his chair. "You want to tell me what's wrong?"

Jess picked up her coffee cup and took a sip of the cold liquid before answering. "No. I don't."

"Something happen in Colorado that I should know about?"

"No."

"Must be a man." Billy sighed. "I've been looking through this music. I don't know if you write better when you're happy or when you're miserable. These latest songs just about break my heart." He studied her carefully neutral expression. "Sure there isn't something I can do? You want me to send him a ticket to Nashville?"

"He wouldn't take it." Jessie turned back to the pages of notes in front of her. "Why don't you tell me what photographer is going to do the cover shots?"

"You'll have to wear a lot of makeup. You look like hell."

"Thanks."

Billy frowned. "You still planning on doing that show in Colorado?"

"Yes. I promised."

"You taking the band?"

"No. I'm going alone. I'll just be gone overnight." Easy in, easy out. She wouldn't look for Dan in the audience, but maybe she could say hello to Anna and Beth. And Grace and Amos. Maybe she could have a cup of coffee at Maizie's before she returned to the airport.

Maybe her heart wouldn't break all over again.

Jessie ignored Billy's concerned expression and pretended to study the music in front of her. She wasn't going to talk about Dan. She didn't want to discuss why she couldn't sleep or eat or make plans for the summer tour. She didn't want to answer questions or think about whether or not to redo the inside of the tour bus. She wanted her music, she wanted Dan and Anna. She wanted to write songs and live in Colorado, and she wasn't going to get her wish.

Dan didn't love her, and there was nothing she could do about that. Like the song said, "I can't make you love me if you don't."

She wished she'd written that song. It sure said it all. She'd loved Dan MacAdams, but she couldn't change who she was or what she did. And he couldn't, either. So that was that. Jess put her hands over her ears to shut out Billy's explanation of cover art and tried not to weep on her future hit song.

"SURE IS LONESOME around here. Pass me the cream, will you?"

Dan passed Amos the pitcher, then turned his attention back to the morning newspaper. The stool to his left, Jessie's place, held an overweight stranger who kept sneezing. Dan gripped the paper higher.

"You heard from her?"

"Heard from who?"

"Jessie."

"No."

"I have," the old man announced proudly. "Just last night."

Dan buried his face deeper into the paper. He'd give everything he owned to hear her voice. "Well, that's good."

"She'll be here on the 23. She's going to arrive in the morning and drive up to Gold City. I offered to pick her up but she didn't want me going to any trouble."

"Nice of her." He put the paper down, knowing he didn't have a chance of reading the football predictions for the weekend. Not with Amos in one of his talkative moods. Not with this ache in his chest, as if someone had punched him. Hard.

"You have your tickets yet? They're goin' like hot-cakes," Amos cackled. "Knew that the little gal would draw a crowd."

Dan scowled. The "little gal" also caused him too many sleepless nights. "Well, that's what she's good at, isn't it?"

"Yep." Amos smacked his lips. "We're rakin' in the bucks on *this* concert. I'm a certified genius, son."

"Yeah. You're a regular brain, Amos." Dan pushed aside his plate and folded up the paper. "And I have to get to work."

"The hotel can't be busy this time of year," the old man declared. "And there's no great emergency that needs your attention, either. This town's been quieter than a church on Saturday night. Have another cup of coffee with me. There's something I need to get off my chest."

Dan didn't want more coffee, or more conversation about Jessie, but he didn't want to hurt his old friend's feelings. He let Maizie refill his cup, then he turned to Amos and waited.

Amos cleared his throat. "I've known you a long time, since you and Wade were kids. I knew your father and your mother and I remember when you got married and when you left and when you came back to town to bury your brother and Susie."

"Amos, I don't—"

The old man held up one gnarled hand. "I know you don't, son. You don't want to talk about the past, and I don't blame you none, but you're a man who has to move on, and I'm the man to tell you it's time to do it."

Dan closed his mouth and waited. He'd let Amos have his say, then he'd go back to the hotel and sit in his office. Correction: in Wade's office. He'd pretend to be working, and he'd try not to think about a gray-eyed blonde with a smile that could knock him to his knees and a voice that wrapped around his heart.

"You let her go." They both knew who he referred to. "Big mistake, in my opinion, but that's neither here nor there." Amos sipped his coffee, as if he was gathering his thoughts. "I buried a wife, too. Same year as you did, and not a day goes by that I don't wish she was with me, nagging me again about wearing my old brown pants."

"She made pretty good oatmeal cookies, I remember."

"Yep. The best." Amos sighed. "Point is, you've got

to get over it. When you get as old as me, you've buried a lot of friends, and most of your family, and a few young ones you didn't expect to go before, if you know what I mean."

Dan nodded, remembering the laughing girl who had worn pink roses in her hair on their wedding day. "I know what you mean."

"You love that little gal singer. Written all over your face every time you looked at her, so don't try to tell me any different," Amos warned. "You should've grabbed the brass ring while you had it in reach, Daniel. You should go get that woman and build another house and have a lot of babies and start making something of your own." Amos eased himself off the stool and clapped the younger man on the shoulder. "Take it from an old man, son, life's too short."

Amos started to pull out his wallet, but Dan stopped him. "Let me get it this time."

Amos nodded his acceptance. "Thanks. I know I'm an interfering old man, but—"

"No," Dan interrupted him, "sometimes I'm a thick-headed fool." He finished his coffee, then walked outside into the cold morning. He pulled his hat low and tugged his collar up to guard against the wind. Main Street was quiet. There would be few tourists now except over the holidays, if the roads stayed open and the skiing was good. They'd have the usual drunk, and someone always went too fast and ended up in a ditch. Dan went back to the hotel and hopped into his car. He drove out of town, up the winding mountain road he'd driven a thousand times, to the house he'd built with a couple of thousand hours of labor. His house, and Carol's.

He parked the car and stepped out into the sunshine. He walked up the hill and stood on the porch that overlooked the valley. Wind brushed the treetops and somewhere a bird complained overhead. There were no ghosts here. Just a foolish man who didn't know how to love or compromise or figure out what the hell he wanted to do with his life. He loved Colorado, loved the mountains and the air and the people. And he loved a woman with music in her heart.

Dan unlocked the door and stepped inside. Jessie had wondered why he didn't live here. He supposed it seemed foolish to hate a house for not being a home, but that's the way he'd felt. He'd resented the hell out of this place for not living up to what he'd envisioned. Just like he'd rejected Jessie for not being the kind of woman he thought he needed. He'd pushed her away, unwilling to risk loving her and losing her.

Jessie Carter had come into his life when he'd been a lonely man, his feelings buried in a grieving heart. She'd brought music and laughter and warmth...and a child. She'd come out of the storm and into his heart and he'd never been the same, no matter how much he tried to pretend he didn't love her.

The lawman stepped carefully through the broken glass and went to the kitchen to find a broom. It was time to move ahead with his life, time to think of the future.

It was time to think of how to get Jessie back.

IT WAS HAPPENING all over again, except this time her hands gripped the wheel of a cherry red four-wheel-drive Jeep, similar to the one she'd left behind in Nashville.

Fat drops of snow pelted the windshield, a challenge to the wipers, already on high speed and having trouble keeping up with the onslaught of snowflakes. Of course, it was December, and she was driving into mountains well-known for their ski slopes, so snow wasn't exactly a surprise.

Jessie wiped the windshield with a gloved hand. The defroster couldn't keep up, either. Still, she didn't consider turning back. She'd promised she'd be there to sing, and she would sing in Gold City, no matter what. She'd brought her gold sequined outfit, the one she usually saved for the second set. She'd brought a thousand-watt amp and an acoustic guitar and she would give a performance they'd never forget.

She'd hold her head high, and she wouldn't let Dan know how much he'd hurt her. From now on, she'd promised herself, her life was hers, her choices hers. And anyone who didn't like it could, well, stick his head in a snowbank.

Jessie chuckled at the thought, her heart light with the decisions she'd made in the past seventy-two hours. She peered through the windshield to make certain she didn't miss the cutoff to Gold City. It couldn't come soon enough. She wanted to be safely ensconced in her room at the Gold Bar before dinner time. She wanted to stride into that hotel and plop her suitcases on the floor and make Dan MacAdams regret ever sending her away.

"WHERE IS SHE?"

"She's most likely held up because of the storm." Grace glanced toward the windows that faced Main Street. "Maybe her plane couldn't land."

"No, it came in. Late, but it's in. I called the airline." Dan paced back and forth in front of the reception desk. The lobby was surprisingly quiet, considering the extra people in town for the concert, and even the lounge didn't sound as boisterous as usual. He wanted a drink.

Grace looked at her watch. "She told me she planned to be here around two. Of course, if her plane was late..."

"She still should have been here by now."

"Unless she had errands to do in Denver."

Dan shot her a disgusted look. "*Errands?*"

Grace shrugged. "Well, it is two days before Christmas."

"No, something's wrong. I can feel it." He swallowed the sudden overwhelming fear in his throat and hurried to his office. "I'm going down the mountain," he called, grabbing his warmest coat from the rack. He picked up a hat, gloves and an extra pair of boots, then took two blankets from the cupboard in the hall.

Grace hurried after him. "Is there anything I can do?"

"You can fix me a flask of brandy and tell Beth I don't know when I'll be by to get Anna. It might be awhile."

It might be more than awhile, he realized as he drove through town. The road was slick; trying to stop at the corner of Main and South was impossible. He drove slowly down the mountain, looking on the side of the road for any signs that someone had skidded into a ditch. He saw no cars on the road; either people had arrived in Gold City earlier in the day, or had decided against driving during a storm.

Was Jessie safe in a motel somewhere? She would have called if she couldn't come. She had promised to be part of the concert and he knew her well enough to know that she would keep her word no matter how dangerous. The damn woman.

He found her after three long miles: a red Jeep wagon stuck sideways and a tiny figure in a blue parka with a shovel in her hand. He would have known her anywhere, and as he parked the car and stepped out into the storm, he saw the stubborn set to her jaw. Yes, he'd know that expression anywhere, too. He tugged on his gloves as he walked to her car.

"You need help?" he called over the wind.

Jessie scooped another shovelful of sand under the rear left tire. "No."

"No?" He grabbed the back of the Jeep to get his balance. Jessie had been busy. Three out of four tires had sand around them, and the fourth was almost done. She'd given herself some traction. "Where'd you learn this?"

She kept shovelling. "I've been up here during a storm once before, remember? I wasn't going to get in another situation where being stupid risked my life."

"Here," he said, taking the shovel, "let me do that."

Jessie kept her grip on the wooden handle. "I'm fine. I don't need any help."

"We're standing in the middle of a damn storm and

half the town is worried about where you are and you sure as hell need help." He took the shovel from her. "I don't want to be out in this any longer than I have to."

"You were looking for me?"

"Yes, damn it. You have a problem with that?"

She didn't reply, just glared at him from under her fluffy blue cap. Her nose was red, and she looked half-frozen.

"There's brandy in my car," he said, hurrying to spread the sand. "And the inside's still warm. Go in there and get warm."

She trudged to his car and went inside. In a few minutes he joined her. She handed him the brandy flask and he took a swallow before speaking.

"It's cold out there."

They both stared out the window. "Think I can make it to town now?" she finally asked. The brandy had warmed her stomach, and she'd finally stopped shivering. She wasn't sorry to see him, but she would have liked to have finished the job herself, just to see if she could. She'd bought an entire emergency kit before she'd headed toward the mountains.

"You should, if you go slow," he replied. "I'd take you with me, but you look like you've got that Jeep packed full. And I can't leave a police vehicle here on the side of the road. I'll have to follow you."

"All right." Jessie turned to him, hoping she could keep pretending she didn't care. He looked wonderful. Warm and solid and safe, and she wanted to throw her arms around him and hug him until the temperature rose ten degrees. She wanted to punch him in the nose for being a fool. "Thanks. I didn't mean to cause you any trouble."

"Lady, you've been giving me trouble since you walked into the diner with that baby." He smiled at her, and Jessie's heart lifted. She knew what that smile meant. He didn't give them often, but when he did the sight warmed her to her toes.

"You deserve it, lawman. You're stubborn and set in your ways and—"

"Crazy in love with you," he finished.

"You've never said it before."

"There are a lot of things I've never said," he admitted. "Like I was a fool to let you walk out years ago. I even shovelled out your truck so you could leave faster."

"I remember. But I don't know if I would have stayed, even if you'd asked me to," she told him. "I wanted to be rich and famous and write hit songs."

"And now?"

"I've decided to take my own advice and live my life the way I want." There was nothing more to prove, she'd realized, thinking of her father. She'd spent a long time proving that she'd been right to leave Chicago, that she'd been a success the only way she knew how.

"I can't go with you," Dan said, pulling her into his arms. He was warm, despite the melting snow on his jacket, and she went willingly into his embrace. "My life is here, with Anna and my work."

"I know that."

"But I've been making some changes, like getting my house ready to live in again."

She lifted her head to look into his eyes. "Really?"

He nodded. "I thought you might need a place to come to, when you're tired of traveling and you need to rest. No more ultimatums, Jess, I promise."

She pulled away from him so she could explain without the distraction of his strong arms around her. "That's not what I want," she said. "I—"

Frustrated, he gripped her shoulders and stared down at her. "Then what the hell *do* you want, Jessie?"

She smiled, which really seemed to confuse him. "Babies," she said. "A husband." His expression cleared. "And a piano. I intend to spend a lot of time doing what I love the most."

"Which is?"

"Writing songs. Taking care of Anna. Having coffee with Amos and tea with Beth."

"Anything else?"

"Making love to you," she added, her voice low.

There was a satisfied gleam in his eyes. "Good idea." He started to pull her toward him again, but she put a gloved hand on his chest to stop him.

"I'll have to go to Nashville once in a while."

Dan nodded. "Yes, I imagine you would."

"And I'll still do concerts," Jessie warned him. "But I'm not going on those long tours anymore. Unless my husband comes with me."

"Husband?" His eyebrows rose.

"Don't tease me, lawman. I'm prepared to buy a house in Gold City and live by myself until you come to your senses and realize you can't live without me."

"I *can't* live without you," Dan stated. He kissed her softly, then added. "I'll have to marry you, I guess. Just to make sure you sing every year at the Christmas concert."

"Is that an official proposal?"

"Yeah." His lips neared hers. "Any problem with that?"

Jessie didn't know it was possible to be this happy, especially with frozen toes and a cold nose. "Only one," she answered.

Dan hesitated, and drew back to look at her. "What?"

"Tell me you love me again."

"I love you." His voice was gruff. "How was that?"

Jessie wrapped her arms around his neck and pulled him closer. "Best lyrics I ever heard, lawman."

# *Harlequin Romance*®

**D**elightful
**A**ffectionate
**R**omantic
**E**motional

**T**ender
**O**riginal

**D**aring
**R**iveting
**E**nchanting
**A**dventurous
**M**oving

*Harlequin Romance*® —
*capturing the world you dream of...*

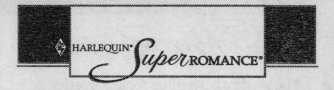

# HARLEQUIN *Presents*

The world's bestselling romance series...
The series that brings you your favorite authors,
month after month:

Helen Bianchin...Emma Darcy
Lynne Graham...Penny Jordan
Miranda Lee...Sandra Marton
Anne Mather...Carole Mortimer
Susan Napier...Michelle Reid

## and many more uniquely talented authors!

Wealthy, powerful, gorgeous men...
Women who have feelings just like your own...
The stories you love, set in exotic, glamorous locations...

# HARLEQUIN *Presents*

## Seduction and passion guaranteed!

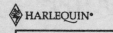

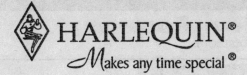

# HARLEQUIN®
## *Makes any time special*®

**HARLEQUIN**®
AMERICAN *Romance*

Upbeat,
All-American Romances

**HARLEQUIN**®
*Duets*™

Romantic Comedy

***Harlequin*® *Historical***

Historical,
Romantic Adventure

HARLEQUIN®
INTRIGUE

Romantic Suspense

*Harlequin Romance*®

Capturing the World
You Dream Of

**HARLEQUIN**® *Presents*~

Seduction and passion
guaranteed

**HARLEQUIN**® *Super*ROMANCE®

Emotional,
Exciting, Unexpected

**HARLEQUIN**® *Temptation*

Sassy, Sexy, Seductive!